His heart ...

The dorsal fin of a shark was slicing through the sea toward Zoe, its sleek body looking like a live torpedo. Benito grabbed a spear gun, his heart thudding.

"Zoe," Benito called. "Start moving toward the ship. Don't get in my sight line."

She began to inch closer to the vessel, her eyes never leaving the shark.

Benito kept the gun trained, his finger on the trigger. When Zoe was only about two yards from the hull, the shark turned and headed away.

Benito felt an incredible rush of relief. Then, in the split second before he reached out a hand to Zoe, that fin sliced around.

In the clear water, Benito could see the shark's savage jaws agape, its dagger-sharp teeth exposed, its eyes rolling back.... And it was racing directly at them.

ABOUT THE AUTHOR

Born in Winnipeg, Manitoba, Dawn Stewardson came to Toronto to attend graduate school and decided Thomas Wolfe was right. She lives on the shore of Lake Ontario with her husband, John, a garden that thinks it's a jungle, and an assortment of animals—many of which have appeared as characters in her books.

Books by Dawn Stewardson

HARLEQUIN INTRIGUE
80—PERIL IN PARADISE
90—NO RHYME OR REASON

HARLEQUIN SUPERROMANCE
405—PRIZE PASSAGE
409—HEARTBEAT
432—THREE'S COMPANY
477—MOON SHADOW
498—ACROSS THE MISTY
521—COLD NOSES, WARM KISSES

Cat and Mouse

Dawn Stewardson

Harlequin Books

TORONTO • NEW YORK • LONDON
AMSTERDAM • PARIS • SYDNEY • HAMBURG
STOCKHOLM • ATHENS • TOKYO • MILAN
MADRID • WARSAW • BUDAPEST • AUCKLAND

To my parents, who like intrigues.
And to John, always.

Harlequin Intrigue edition published April 1993

ISBN 0-373-22222-X

CAT AND MOUSE

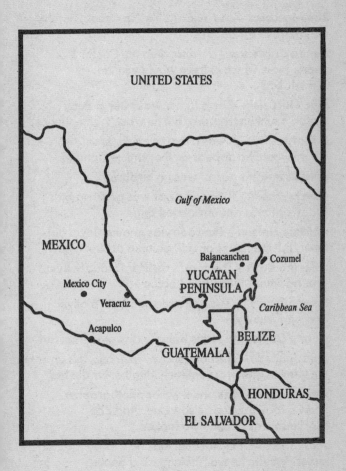

CAST OF CHARACTERS

Zoe MacLeish—Zoe means "life" in Greek, but she was marked for death.

Benito Cardenas—He'd tracked the Cat for three years. Now which of them would win the showdown?

Mac MacLeish—Zoe's father was after *El Poco Grifon's* sunken treasure, but he wasn't the only one.

El Gato—The Cat was a master of disguise. As whom would he appear on the *Yankee Doodle?*

Billy Bird—This parrot was no birdbrain.

Marco Vinelli—The head diver was growing old. Was he after a retirement nest egg?

Chicken Nelson—The cook was another loyal old-timer, but the finger of guilt pointed at him twice.

Jake the Rake—The cook's assistant was always around when "accidents" occurred.

Sandy Braukis—The first mate had both motive and opportunity.

Danny Doyle—Was this friendly diver too friendly?

Sam Johnson—The newest crew member, this diver had the least to gain from untimely deaths. Or did he?

Dean Cooper—The underwater photographer knew a looker when he saw one. And Zoe MacLeish was definitely a looker.

Justo Diaz—Of the local divers, he was by far the nicest. Maybe he was looking for a bonus.

John Medeiros—Filmmaker or widow maker?

Prologue

"I'm not going along with it, Lopez," Mac said. "Absolutely, definitely not."

"You surprise me, Señor MacLeish. After your unhappy experience in South America, I expected you would be more eager for a license to salvage in Mexican waters once more."

Mac gritted his teeth and stared out into the yellow smog that passed for air in Mexico City. The story of his getting shafted down in that banana republic had certainly made the rounds. And every time someone mentioned it, his blood pressure jumped.

Damned revolutionaries. They'd overthrown the old government while he was in the middle of operations, then confiscated every last item his divers had retrieved. Instead of a fortune, the *Yankee Doodle* had sailed away with nothing.

He focused on Lopez again, saying that he *was* eager for the license. "Very eager," he added. "But if there's one thing thirty years in the business has taught me, it's that there's enough danger in underwater work without begging for more. And your setting up some half-baked sting operation could attract every crackpot in the Caribbean."

Miguel Lopez raised his pudgy hands, palms up, and slowly shrugged. "Señor MacLeish, I have explained our proposition. As you Americans say, take it or leave it."

"Dammit," Mac snapped, "your government already gets any of the artifacts it wants. Plus half of whatever else we retrieve."

"*Sí,* the customary salvage agreement."

"Well, the rest sure as hell isn't customary. Asking me to endanger my crew and ship is asking too damned much."

"Señor MacLeish, it is exactly because of the danger that we hesitate to grant you a license. What if your *Yankee Doodle* was to come to harm?"

"Come to harm? Let's not mince words, Lopez. You mean, what if my ship was to *mysteriously* explode."

"*Sí,* it is what I mean precisely. Ships exploding, killing the crew, injuring Americans on a nearby yacht. Things of that sort frighten the tourists from coming to Mexico. One incident like the *Pegasus* can be explained as an unfortunate accident. But two? Perhaps more?"

"Lopez, what happened to the *Pegasus* isn't going to happen again. Before those guys blew her up, they took enough gold off her to last them a lifetime. They wouldn't risk sticking around and trying a repeat performance. Not with everyone waiting and watching for them to."

"It is not so much *those guys,* Señor MacLeish. And perhaps you are right about them not sticking around. They were...how do you say in English...ahh, hired help, that is all they were. But the man who planned the crime, he has given us much trouble. He has stolen fortunes before. On land. And our information says he will now try another salvage ship."

"Hell," Mac muttered, "he'd be crazy to. Every salvor in the Caribbean knows the *Pegasus* didn't have any *accident*. I'll bet your mastermind's retired to the French Riviera or someplace. And wherever he is, he's probably planning to stay put for the rest of his life."

"Perhaps. And since you believe that, it will be no problem for you to cooperate with us, *sí?*"

"Cooperate with you? You sure use interesting turns of phrase, Lopez. What you're really asking me to do is play decoy while you try to lure this guy into your net."

"No, Señor MacLeish. We will do nothing to lure. So you have no reason to fear those crackpots you spoke of. But if our suspect has *not* retired to the French Riviera, he may...what is the word...surface? Is that right?"

"Yeah, surface is right," Mac snapped. Bad enough he was being manipulated. He could certainly live without giving English lessons.

"So," Lopez continued calmly, "when we announce we are granting you a license to salvage *El Poco Grifon*, when it is known she carried a gold cargo worth...how much do you say?"

"Fifty million," Mac supplied, glancing out the window again to hide his annoyance. That officious little twerp knew exactly what the treasure was worth. One thing those early Spaniards did was keep precise cargo manifests.

"Fifty million dollars," Lopez said. "That is much money. So, if our criminal is still in Mexico, he will be most interested in it, *sí?* And Señor MacLeish?"

When Mac looked back across the desk, Lopez said quietly, "Was not the captain of the *Pegasus* a friend of yours?"

"Yes...Carl Medeiros was a good friend. We went way back—both started salvaging in the Greek islands when we were young."

"And all I am asking, is for you to help us arrest the man who has murdered your friend. All I am asking is for you to have an agent from the Policia Federale on board your *Yankee Doodle*, watching for our suspect."

"Dammit, Lopez, I can watch for him myself. And if he shows up, I can take care of him myself."

Lopez slowly shrugged again. "Señor MacLeish, your friend could not take care of him."

"Carl didn't even know the guy existed. I do."

"That is true. But we are talking about a clever and dangerous man. A salvage license for *El Poco Grifon* will be given only to a captain who is willing to cooperate. And now that you have so kindly pointed to where the wreck must lie, I am sure we can find many such a captain."

Mac jammed his hands into his pockets, trying to calm down and think. There was absolutely no doubt that the few artifacts they'd already recovered had been aboard the *Grifon* when she sank. That made him certain they could pinpoint the wreck in no time flat.

He couldn't simply sail away from the biggest treasure he'd ever had a shot at. Not when his own daughter's research had started him on this search. Not when everyone involved in the venture—from his investors to the last man on his crew—had a stake in the treasure. But he sure didn't relish Lopez turning the *Yankee Doodle* into a sitting duck.

Of course, if this mastermind actually *was* still around, the *Yankee* might be a sitting duck, anyway. Which meant he'd have to make damned sure a certain someone stayed in California.

But hell, he'd really love to help nail the bastard who killed Carl. And if agreeing to have an agent aboard was the only way of getting the license . . . well, what could it hurt? He considered for another moment, then said, "Who's the guy you figure was behind hitting the *Pegasus*?"

"A thief of artifacts and ancient treasure. The *federales* have been after him for maybe three years. But still he is known to them only as El Gato."

"El Gato. The Cat."

"*Sí*, the cat who disappears into the night." Lopez held his thumb and forefinger a fraction apart, saying, "The *federales* were this close to catching him when he plundered the ruins of Kohunlich. Then he vanished. And now he reappears to steal treasure from the water instead of the pyramids."

"El Gato," Mac said again. "And you don't even know his real identity."

"No, but we will soon. With your help . . . or that of some other captain."

Chapter One

She was going to strangle him. She was going to climb aboard that ship, wrap her hands around his throat and strangle him.

Zoe's pilot, a boy of ten or eleven, kept glancing uneasily at her, so she told herself to stop muttering. But she *was* going to strangle her father. And the way this catamaran was skimming along, he had only about five minutes more to live.

They'd quickly left the island of Cozumel behind. And ahead, across the sparkling Caribbean, the Yucatán Peninsula's eastern coastline was growing hazily visible. Directly before them, anchored above the sand bars that eighteenth-century Spaniards had called the Perfido Shoals, lay the *Yankee Doodle*.

She gazed across the water at it, loving every inch of its hundred and forty feet. Most salvage ships looked more like ugly, rusty tugs than anything else, but the *Yankee Doodle* was a lot like Cousteau's *Calypso*—a gleaming white beauty.

Usually, seeing it for the first time each spring started her heart racing. Today, her initial glimpse had simply made her blood boil faster.

Zoe caught her pilot's attention and told him in Spanish to head for the ladder near the stern.

"*Sí, señorita,*" he said, adjusting the rudder slightly.

She eyed the ship as they drew nearer, noting she was in luck. The divers must be working, because the gate at the top of the ladder was hooked open. At least she wouldn't have to haul herself over the side.

Her pint-size pilot brought them in directly beside the ladder—so close to the ship that each lapping wave brushed the cat against the *Yankee Doodle*'s steel hull.

Zoe smiled at the child, doubting she could have done as well. "*Muy bien,*" she said, scrambling to her feet and handing him an adult-size tip that made him grin.

She shrugged into her backpack, gave the bottom of her shorts a quick tug, then grasped the sides of the ladder and swung onto it.

"*Más tarde, señorita,*" her pilot called, deftly catching the breeze once more. He turned the cat back in the direction of Cozumel as Zoe started up the side of the ship.

Halfway to the top a shadow fell across her and she glanced up. Backlit by the sunlight's glare, the dark shape of a man was looming over her.

She climbed a couple of more rungs then stopped, her face level with a pair of bare feet. When they didn't step out of her way, she put one hand above her sunglasses, shading her eyes, and let her gaze trail slowly upward...along bronze male calves...to muscular thighs that eventually disappeared into cut-offs. Extremely short cutoffs. In fact, if he cut off even one more thread, they'd be positively indecent.

Above the faded denim loomed more naked bronze man. His chest wasn't hairy, but that only emphasized the firm delineation of its muscles.

Her gaze reached his face. In the brightness she couldn't see perfectly, but he seemed to be one of those rare Mexicans of almost pure Spanish descent—classically chiseled Latin features that reminded her of the marble statues in the Prado.

Not bad. Not bad at all. Maybe, after she was through killing her father, she'd see if whoever this was had any brains to go with his brawn. Then he spoke and she instantly rejected the idea.

"Sorry," he said, his English perfect, his arrogant tone telling her he wasn't really the least bit sorry. "No unauthorized persons are allowed aboard the *Yankee Doodle*," he added, then unhooked the latch that held the gate open.

Zoe could scarcely believe it. He intended to shut the gate in her face. Did he expect her to swim back to Cozumel?

She pushed her sunglasses onto the top of her head and fixed him with a glare—a difficult feat when he was towering over her and she was looking into the sun, but she did her best. "I am not an unauthorized person," she said icily. "I am Zoe MacLeish. And if you will kindly get out of my way—"

Suddenly, a familiar voice was shrilling her name, there was a flash of blue-and-gold motion against the blue of the sky, and Mr. Bronze Arrogance was hitting the deck, swearing a string of obscenities in Spanish, barely making it out of Billy's flight path in time.

Zoe clung to the ladder more tightly, wishing her T-shirt had padded shoulders, while Billy thudded, as lightly as a large macaw could, onto her shoulder.

"Hi, Billy Bird, I've missed you," she murmured their usual greeting.

"Hi, Zoe," he said, rearranging himself so he was facing the same direction she was. "I've missed you," he added, rubbing her cheek with the side of his head.

While she stepped up onto the deck, the keeper-of-the-gate climbed to his feet—glowering at Billy as if he'd immensely enjoy parrot stew for dinner.

Zoe could feel herself smirking a mile-wide smirk. She made a halfhearted attempt to transform it into an innocent smile, then said sweetly, "You see, even a birdbrain knows I'm not an unauthorized person."

"YOU FINISHED YELLING?" Mac demanded. "Ready to listen?"

Zoe shrugged, not meeting his gaze, pretending to be fascinated by the familiar burnished mahogany of his cabin's walls.

Her anger certainly wasn't dissipated, but she was already feeling guilty about not greeting her father with her customary hugs and kisses. She adored him, and every time she saw him after months apart, she felt a little surge of relief that he was the same as ever.

His blue eyes still sparkled with a glint that said he could take on half a dozen comers and beat them without breathing hard. He might look every one of his fifty-five years—a lifetime in the elements and his mane of gray hair ensured that—but he was a hulk of a man and his work kept him fit.

She put the newspaper clipping she'd been waving under his nose onto the desk, and said that yes, she was ready to listen.

"Good," Mac muttered, reaching past her and picking up the clipping. "Damned California papers," he said, "they never get anything right."

"Oh?" Zoe asked suspiciously. Not many people could read expression in that craggy face, but she could. And her father was definitely going to try keeping something from her. "And what didn't that particular article get right?" she said. "*Have* you recovered several items that were aboard *El Poco Grifon* when she sank?"

"No, not several. Only four."

"Four. But they *were* conclusively identified as being from the *Grifon*?"

Mac nodded with obvious reluctance.

"And they *were* enough to convince the government to give you the salvage license, weren't they?" she pressed.

"Well . . . yeah, that bit's right."

"I see. And how about the part that says you've virtually pinpointed the location of the wreck?"

"Nope. They're way off base there. We haven't found it yet."

"*Virtually located*, Dad. It doesn't say found, it says virtually located."

"Zoe, I promised I'd let you know as soon as we found it."

"Oh, no, that isn't what you promised at all. You said you'd phone me again the instant things started to get exciting. But you said that only three days ago, when things were apparently *already* darned exciting. Dad, why were you telling me *nothing* was happening? Convincing me I should sit tight in California and finish my dull old thesis, when you're about to raise the treasure? What on earth are you up to?''

Mac stood watching her intently, finally saying, ''Look, your being aboard right now would give me a problem with accommodations. I've got a guy bunking in your cabin.''

''Oh, come off it! You can't move him out?''

''Well . . . look, baby, the blunt truth is that I don't want you here.''

''What?'' she shrieked.

''Dammit, Zoe, lower your voice or the whole damned crew will hear you.''

''I don't care if the whole damned Caribbean hears me! If it hadn't been for the information *I* happened across during my thesis research, if it hadn't been for *my* poring over all those records in that dusty old archive in Seville, you wouldn't even have a clue where *El Poco Grifon* sank, let alone have virtually pinpointed her location. And now you don't want me here?''

''Zoe, I—''

''Fat chance of keeping me away, Dad! Fat chance.''

''Dammit, Zoe, aren't archaeology professors supposed to be quiet and mild mannered? Like librarians? And aren't female ones supposed to wear their hair in buns?'' he added, glancing critically at her long tangle of dark hair.

She ignored the glance. If he wasn't so darned stubborn, he'd have long ago given up hoping she'd ever turn into what he called a ''proper lady.''

''I am not,'' she reminded him stiffly, ''a professor yet. I'm a mere lecturer until my thesis is finished. And even then, I'll only be an assistant professor. And you know I'll never in a million years be quiet and mild mannered. Or wear my hair in a bun.''

Mac shook his head, saying, ''It's just as well you live in California, isn't it? Where the abnormal is normal. You know, Zoe, every now and then I wish you'd inherited your mother's placid nature along with her good looks.''

''Well, I didn't. I might not look like you, but there's sure no doubting I'm your daughter, is there? And you don't have a snowball's hope in hell of getting me off this ship. Why on earth don't you want me here?'' she demanded.

''Baby...look, I didn't mean that to come out sounding quite the way it did. You know I love having you here. Hell, you haven't missed a summer aboard the *Yankee* since you stopped living on her year-round.''

''You mean since you banished me, kicking and screaming, to boarding school when I was thirteen.''

''Zoe, let's not get into that old one again. Your living aboard ship was all right while your mother was alive, but after she died I wasn't doing such a hot job of bringing you up, and—''

''You were doing just fine.''

''Well, once the crew started noticing you weren't exactly a little girl anymore...besides, I wanted you to get a good education, and—''

''And I did,'' she interrupted, trying to avoid his lengthy ''a salvage ship is no place for a woman'' lecture. She'd never been entirely sure he was right about that, but spending May through August on the *Yankee* each year had turned out to be an acceptable compromise for both of them. And there was no way he was going to change the ground rules on her this summer.

"Dad," she continued quickly, "I get to use that good education you paid for when I'm with you. Why do you think I specialized in *marine* archaeology? And the college looks on it as my doing field work—and that gets me brownie points with them."

"I know, Zoe. But this particular summer...I'm just worried about your being aboard ship right now."

"Why?"

Mac ran his fingers through his hair, finally saying, "Remember I told you about the *Pegasus* explosion?"

"Of course. I felt terrible about Carl Medeiros being killed."

"Well, the thing is, it's possible that explosion wasn't an accident. And just in case...maybe I'm being overprotective, but just in case, I'd really rather you went back to California."

"*Maybe* you're being overprotective? Dad, I'm a responsible, twenty-seven-year-old woman. And just because it's *possible* the explosion wasn't an accident..." She paused, realizing what the point was, and asked, "If it wasn't an accident, what happened?"

"There's just a rumor going around, Zoe. It isn't worth repeating."

She waited for her father to tell her this was all simply a warped joke. When he didn't, she said, "A rumor. You think I should leave because of a rumor that isn't even worth repeating? How about repeating it and letting me judge for myself."

Mac eyed her with obvious annoyance for a minute, then said, "All right, it's more than a rumor. The explosion definitely wasn't any accident. Some gang of modern-day pirates boarded the *Pegasus,* tied up the crew, snatched the treasure Carl had raised, then blew the ship out of the water with a damned remote explosive."

"Oh..." She hadn't been quite prepared for the truth—not that particular truth, at least.

"And you're worried it might happen to the *Yankee,*" she finally said.

"No," Mac said, shaking his head. "Not really."

She felt a tiny wave of relief at his words, but it was too tiny to entirely wash away her concern. If there was even the slightest chance of something happening to the *Yankee*—to her father—the last thing in the world she'd do was go back to California. She'd stay right here and see for herself that everything was fine.

"Zoe," Mac said, "I just worry about you."

"Oh, Daddy, if you don't really believe anything's going to happen, then don't worry about me, okay? And give me a hug. And forget I yelled at you."

Mac made a circle of his arms and she rushed into it, whispering, "I love you, Daddy."

"I love you, too, baby," he said gruffly.

She gave him a long, hard hug before drawing away. "I saw you've got a new crew member," she said, quickly latching on to an innocuous subject. Displays of affection often made her father uncomfortable.

"I've got several new crew members," he told her. "I've got five local divers coming aboard from Cozumel every morning. We *do* almost have the *Grifon* pinpointed, Zoe. And I want to zero in and start getting her treasure up top as fast as I can."

She nodded. To move quickly was only sensible. The longer a salvage took to get going, the more risk of a storm blowing up and disturbing the bottom. That could mean having to redo a lot of the work.

"You're usually so picky about your crew, though," she said after a moment. "And the guy I met was a total jerk."

"Who was he?" Mac said.

"I didn't ask his name. But he doesn't look like a run-of-the-mill diver. He's in his early thirties. Tall, dark and..." And for some ridiculous reason, the word *handsome* almost popped out. "And he speaks perfect English. In an obnoxiously know-it-all tone, though," she concluded.

"That must have been Benito Cárdenas," Mac said. "His parents have money—sent him off to school in the States from the time he was a kid. And from what I've seen, it practically turned him into an American."

"Oh," Zoe said. Maybe she shouldn't have judged Mr. Bronze Arrogance quite so harshly. If he was native Mexican, looked Spanish, and had spent a lot of his life in America, could be his problem wasn't entirely his fault—might have something to do with induced schizophrenia.

"But he's never used an obnoxiously know-it-all tone with *me*," Mac went on. "And he's certainly not a diver. He's an archaeologist."

Zoe pictured those long muscular legs, that broad expanse of chest, and said he didn't look like an archaeologist. "I mean," she added, "unless you're going to count Harrison Ford playing Indiana Jones."

"Well, baby, we were just saying that you don't look like an archaeologist, either, weren't we? At any rate, Ben's an examiner for the Archives of Mexico. He's aboard to look out for the government's interests—

assess the artifacts we retrieve as to their...how the hell do those guys phrase it...oh yeah, he assesses their intrinsic archaeological value."

"In other words," Zoe said, "he's the one who decides what the government takes and what you get to keep."

"Right. And I don't want him deciding the whole damned treasure's of intrinsic archaeological value, so don't go getting off on the wrong foot with him, huh?"

"Who, me?" Zoe said.

BENITO CÁRDENAS sat on the edge of his berth, watching Mac pace the small confines of the cabin and hoping to hell that woman's arrival wasn't going to throw a wrench into the works.

Almost all he knew about archaeology was what he remembered from a few courses way back in his university days. If he kept his mouth shut most of the time, he might manage to fake out the crew, but he wasn't going to fool the captain's daughter.

Of the thousands of possible occupations, why did Zoe MacLeish have to be a marine archaeologist? Maybe he could manage to get by for the moment, but as soon as the divers began bringing up artifacts she'd realize he was a fraud.

Hell, he should have heaved her back off the ship the moment she set foot on deck—and tossed that fool bird Mac, called a watch-parrot, along with her. But since he hadn't, he'd have to figure out how he was going to handle things when she put two and two together.

Right now, though, he'd better find out what Mac was thinking. "You know," he said casually, "I wish you'd mentioned having a daughter who might show up. With El Gato's reputation as a master of disguise, I figured that could have been *him* climbing the ladder."

"Good God," Mac said. "Don't ever tell Zoe you thought she was a criminal in drag. She'd kill you."

Benito smiled wryly, thinking the woman could likely kill with nothing more than that sharp tongue of hers. She might look like an angel, but she was clearly a walking, talking example of looks being deceiving.

"Ben, I hated lying to her about you," Mac went on. "I understand why you don't want anyone knowing you're actually with the *federales,* but I think we should at least tell Zoe."

"No, you did the right thing. She could let it slip, so let's keep it from her as long as we can."

Mac paced the narrow breadth of the cabin again and stood staring out the window.

"I just don't know what to do about this," he finally said, turning back. "Her arriving like that surprised me so much I didn't have a chance to think. I hardly knew what to say. Maybe I shouldn't have told her the truth about the *Pegasus.*"

"I can't see you had much choice, Mac."

"Yeah...having her aboard changes things, though. The crew and I can take care of ourselves, but Zoe..."

Benito swore silently. From what little he'd seen, he doubted Zoe MacLeish had any problems taking care of herself. But if Mac was worried it was bound to show. And El Gato could spot a trap a mile away.

"Dammit," Mac muttered, "short of tying Zoe up, there's no way I'm going to get her off this ship. So how about us putting our plan on hold? I'll just make sure we don't locate the main wreck until after she's gone. She can't stay past the end of August. She has to teach the fall term.''

"Uh-uh. Holding off isn't feasible, Mac. Hiring those extra divers said loud and clear that you expect to locate the *Grifon* any day now. So if we didn't start things moving, El Gato would get suspicious. And he's gotten away with too much, for too long, to chance losing him again.''

"Ben . . . look, I know I made a deal, but I'm not going to risk having my only child blown to kingdom come.''

"That's the one thing we don't have to worry about. There's no way El Gato would try to blow up the *Yankee Doodle*.''

"No? Well, maybe you're right. That's what I figured back when Lopez sucked me into going along with this idea. But what if we're both wrong?''

"Mac, I've been after El Gato for almost three years, I've learned how he thinks. And blowing up the *Pegasus* was simply his way of announcing his first hit on a ship.''

"Announcing it with a bang, so to speak,'' Mac muttered.

"But there won't be a bang next time, Mac. The main reason we haven't gotten El Gato is that he never uses the same MO twice.''

The captain looked skeptical. "If that's true, then how do you know which crimes he's responsible for?''

"You should have been a detective.''

"I'm happy being a salvor, but my question stands.''

"Well, whenever El Gato's behind a hit, he lets us know. He's one of those criminals who's certain he's smarter than we are, and wants to rub it in. So he leaves a memento at each scene to taunt us, kind of a calling card."

"What kind?"

"It varies. But it's always something he took during his previous crime."

Mac nodded slowly, then said, "What about the *Pegasus*? How could he leave something behind when the scene was a patch of Caribbean Sea?"

"Good question. With that one, he let us know afterward that he was responsible. A couple of months before the *Pegasus*, he hit some Mayan ruins—the Kohunlich ruins in Quintana Roo."

"Yeah, Lopez mentioned something about that."

"Well, he got a lot of gold and jewelry from one of the tombs, but something puzzled me at the time. He left behind an emerald earring that was pretty valuable. Turned out he had his reason, though. The day after the *Pegasus* blew, a package was delivered to headquarters. Inside was an emerald earring—the mate to the one at Kohunlich."

"And?" Mac said.

"And it was wrapped in the front page of a newspaper, a front page devoted entirely to the *Pegasus* story."

Mac nodded slowly. "So there's no doubt it was your Cat."

"None at all."

"And you figure, if he tries to hit another salvage ship, his method will be different."

"Definitely."

"That sure makes me feel a helluva lot better," Mac muttered. "There can't be more than a few thousand other things he could try. Look, Ben, I'm between the proverbial rock and hard place. I don't want trouble with Zoe aboard. But I can't back off of this salvage—not after that fiasco in South America."

Benito watched the captain curiously and waited for him to elaborate.

He shook his head, muttering, "I thought the whole world knew that story. Lopez didn't tell you what happened?"

"Uh-uh."

"Well, we got robbed blind down there. I had a standard salvage agreement with the government in power—was entitled to half of what we raised. And it was one of the fastest operations I'd ever lucked into. Only a few months and we were almost done. Then there was a coup, and those jerks who formed the *new* government grabbed the entire treasure.

"Hell, Ben, we were all almost rich men and it disappeared from under our noses. So the crew are really counting on their share from the *Grifon*. But I can't have anything happen to Zoe—even if it isn't being blown to smithereens."

"Mac, we're not *certain* El Gato's even going to try something."

"No?" the captain said doubtfully.

"All right, I'll be totally straight with you, Mac. After Lopez announced granting you the license, some guy showed up in the Museum of Anthropology, wanting to see the records they have on shipwrecks...particularly those in 1724."

"The year the *Grifon* sank."

"Exactly. Anyway, this guy claimed he was a professor at the University of Mexico. But after he'd left, the curator started thinking something hadn't been quite right and checked him out. The University had never heard of the man."

"El Gato," Mac said.

"We think so. But he sure isn't going to take us by surprise. That makes all the difference in the world. And as far as Zoe's safety is concerned, I know you'd be keeping a close watch on her. And look, if it'll make you feel better, I'll stick to her like glue."

He waited for Mac's reaction, thinking that if he stuck close to Zoe she'd realize all the faster he was a fraud. But if baby-sitting her was what it would take to convince Mac...

The captain was a hard man to read, but he looked as if he was still undecided. "Mac, I had a lot of experience protecting people when I first became an agent. And I never lost one."

"Never?"

"Never even came close."

"And you'd stick to her like glue, huh?"

"You've got my word on it."

"She wouldn't like that, Ben. She's a free spirit."

"Mac, she wouldn't have to like it. But how far could she get from me on a hundred-and-forty-foot ship?"

Benito waited again, knowing he'd live to regret his offer. The only question was how much he'd regret it. His brief encounter with Zoe MacLeish had been enough to tell him they were fire and ice.

"All right," Mac finally said, "you stick to her and we'll still got a deal."

Benito smiled, saying, "Good."

"Just one thing."

"What's that?"

"This is Zoe's cabin I gave you, and I don't want you getting any ideas about sticking *that* close to her. You'll have to move your gear to the crew quarters.

"And Ben," he added, opening the door, "one more thing. Something I want clear between us, man to man. If anything does happen to my little girl, I'll kill you."

"I DON'T LIKE THIS," the shorter man said, leaning against the *Yankee*'s rail. He was trying to look casual, but his insides were churning so hard he could taste bile in the back of his throat.

"Relax, Tonto," his partner said.

That made him smile a little. Of all the nicknames he'd had in his life, he liked Tonto the best. And when his buddy had come up with it, he'd started calling him the Lone Ranger in return, and that's what they'd called each other ever since.

But this wasn't any time to be smiling and thinking about nicknames. "I don't like her coming here and all of a sudden things are more complicated," he pressed.

The Lone Ranger merely stared out across the blue water.

"The captain's one thing," he persisted, "but a woman? Even if it wasn't Zoe...see, I don't know if I can stomach killing a woman."

That earned him a scornful glance. "You been living in a cave for the past twenty years, Tonto? Women get treated equal these days. Besides, I don't recall you having any qualms when I was arranging the contract on her."

"That was different. Paying some stranger to kill her in California, and having to do the job ourselves—right under the old man's nose—are real different things."

"Dead is dead," the Lone Ranger said. "Besides, this way, we won't have to pay for it."

"But we'll have to do it. How we gonna do it? You figure out a plan?"

"Not yet, but I will. We'll make it look like an accident . . . not make the captain suspicious."

Tonto heard a murmur of voices along the deck and turned toward the bow. It was her, talking to that Mexican government dude, and just looking at her made him more worried.

He glanced back at the Lone Ranger and said he still didn't like it. "Couldn't we just scare her off the ship?" he suggested. "Let that contract stand? Then, when she goes back home . . ."

"There isn't time for that. Hey, man, I'm getting real tired of listening to you whine. You want out, Tonto?"

He looked at Zoe again, wishing he knew how risky it would be, thinking how much money was involved, finally saying, "No, I don't want out. I'm still in."

"Fine. Then shut the hell up about what you don't like. You know what we have to do, Tonto. First we get the daughter. Then we get the father. Then we get the loot."

Chapter Two

The morning sun had climbed halfway to its noon position, and even out on the water the day was steamy. Above, a frigate bird glided lazily over the ship.

It was *definitely* too hot to be out on deck. But with Mac diving, Benito was stuck watching Zoe. Watching her while pretending he wasn't. Because from the moment she'd climbed aboard yesterday, she'd made it clear she wanted nothing to do with him. Now she stood gazing out over the water—her arms resting on the rail, that ornery watch-parrot perched beside her.

Up on the observation platform, above the bridge, the tall and skinny cook's assistant everyone called Jake the Rake was standing watch. With only seven permanent crew aside from Mac, everyone except old Chicken Nelson, the cook, pulled his weight on deck as well as having a specific job.

But *his* specific job on the *Yankee*, Benito thought, was supposed to be catching El Gato—not playing nursemaid to the captain's daughter.

And right now he was itching to be underwater, down seeing what those five temporary divers from Cozumel were up to. If El Gato was going to try infiltrating the *Yankee,* putting one of those divers on his payroll would be a likely way to do it.

Benito's gaze drifted back to Zoe. She was as ornery as the damned bird, but he'd admit she was a good-looking woman. Tall, slender, wild black hair the breeze kept blowing sexily about, big green eyes, and what might possibly be the shapeliest long legs he'd ever seen . . .

He was still admiring her legs when Dean Cooper, the underwater photographer, appeared from below deck and sauntered in Zoe's direction.

The instant he joined her at the rail, Billy Bird made a rude, screeching noise, treated him to a few menacing flaps of his big blue wings, then flew off up to the observation platform.

Cooper edged a little closer to Zoe.

The way she immediately moved away made Benito grin. He wasn't the only one she'd decided rated an icy shoulder.

She leaned out over the rail, and a minute later Mac appeared at the top of the ladder, his mask shoved up on his head and water dripping from his gray hair.

While Mac swung himself onto the deck and began shrugging out of his scuba tank, Benito started over. As far as everyone but the captain was concerned, Señor Benito Cárdenas was with the national archives, so he'd better express some interest in how the search was going.

"Anything promising yet?" Zoe was asking when he reached the three of them.

"It's got to be right around here someplace," Mac said. "But the shifting sand is a good twenty feet deep down there, so . . . well, you know how it is. We just have to keep searching through it until we start hitting pay dirt.''

"You have any idea how spread out the treasure's going to be?'' Dean Cooper said. "I'm okay for stills, but if we're going to need a lot of long pan shots, I should get extra videotape.''

"Zoe did some sketches of what she figures the site will be like,'' Mac told him. "Baby, I've got work to do on the bridge, so you let Cooper have a look at them, huh? You'd be interested, too, Ben.''

"They're in my cabin,'' Zoe said. "I'll get them and meet the two of you in the lounge, okay?'' She turned and headed toward the forward cabins, mentally berating her father for sticking her with that pair of clowns.

Every so often, some character came along who considered the presence of a female aboard ship as a personal challenge. And this time she'd hit double jeopardy—Dean Cooper and Benito Cárdenas.

It had taken her all of thirty seconds to peg Dean Cooper. He should have On the Make permanently tattooed on his forehead. But she must be losing her edge, because she hadn't picked up on Benito Cárdenas as quickly.

When he'd tried to keep her off the ship, using that imperious manner of his, she could have cheerfully kicked him. And she'd thought the instant dislike was mutual. Since then, though, he seemed to be everywhere she went, and he'd barely taken his eyes off her.

She didn't know which was worse—Mr. Bronze-Arrogance-Government-Archaeologist or Mr. Big-Blond-Hungry-Eyed-Photographer. What she did know was that every time she turned around, one or the other of those two seemed to be breathing down her neck.

"So, dummy," she told herself, opening her cabin door, "the solution's simple. Stop turning around."

She began sorting through the drawings, then paused and buzzed the galley to ask Chicken Nelson if he still had coffee on. Benito and Dean might be easier to take with a strong dose of caffeine.

"Zoe," Chicken muttered through the intercom, "I've been your father's cook longer than you've been alive. And when have you ever known me not to have the..." He paused, noisily swallowing a word, then added, "not to have the coffee on?"

"Sorry, should have remembered you're perfect, Chicken," she told him, smiling to herself. The crew always tried to clean up their language while she was aboard. But sooner or later, somebody was going to choke, keeping back one of those swear words they were normally so free with.

SKETCHES IN HAND, Zoe hurried down the steep metal staircase that led from the forward deck to the combination lounge and dining area.

She could see Benito and Dean sitting on the lounge side, but by spreading the drawings out on the dining table she'd be able to make this meeting a quick one.

On the way to her cabin, she'd noticed someone on the observation platform, relieving Jake the Rake from watch duty. So Jake would be coming down here pretty soon, wanting to set up for lunch.

Yes, using the table was definitely a good idea, she decided, reaching the bottom step. Then her foot hit the wooden floor and kept right on moving.

Suddenly she was airborne.

The next instant she was landing flat on her back.

There was a dull thud and every ounce of air rushed from her body.

The sketches were flying through the air; the room was spinning around her. Her head was pounding, her backside hurt like hell, and both Benito and Dean were thundering toward her.

All she could think of was the running of the bulls in Pamplona. She was about to be trampled and finished off completely.

Miraculously, both men managed to stop before that happened. They dropped to the floor beside her, Dean saying, "You all right, Zoe?"

Lord, she thought dizzily, here they were, both breathing down her neck at once now. And this time, she hadn't even turned around.

"Don't touch her," Benito snapped when Dean grabbed her arms and started to pull her up. "She might have broken something. Zoe, lie perfectly still," he added, lifting her head and examining the back of it.

She didn't think anything was more than bruised, but didn't think she was up to an argument, either. So she simply lay there—her pride hurting as much as either her head or backside—and tried not to imagine how ridiculous her flying entrance had looked.

Then Benito found a sore spot and she winced.

He checked it more closely. "A bump's forming," he reported, "but there's no blood." He peered into her eyes and held a hand in front of her face. "How many fingers do you see?"

She counted eight, thought hard about it for a second, and said, "Four."

"Tell me the date."

That took even more thought, but she'd left California on the fifth, so... "May 6."

"What year?"

"Sixteen hundred and two," she told him sarcastically. Enough was enough. "I'm going to live, Benito. I promise."

He seemed to look somewhat relieved at that news, but she wasn't really sure. She definitely had a case of fuzzy double vision.

"God," he muttered, "you could have broken your neck. And if your head had hit those metal steps...just a good thing it didn't. Let's see about the rest of you."

He began poking and pressing her neck and shoulders, his broad chest practically touching her body, his face so close to hers that she could feel the warmth of his breath on her cheek. Then he moved his hands down to her rib cage, and suddenly his touch was most disconcerting.

She tried to push his hands away, struggling to get up, saying, "I'm all right."

"I told you to lie still," he said, unceremoniously shoving her shoulders back flat on the floor. "If you've done any damage, you'll just make it worse by moving around."

She gritted her teeth and lay still, but the way his hands were moving over her body was absolutely mortifying. The two things she hated most in the world were being manhandled and being told what to do. And Benito was managing both at once. No wonder she didn't like him.

Just as she decided her face must be the color of an overripe tomato, he said, "Okay, you seem to be in one piece." He helped her to her feet, his arm wrapped securely around her shoulders.

She considered shrugging it off, but if she did that she'd probably fall flat on her face. She needed a minute to steady herself—might even need a minute and a half.

"Feel dizzy?" Dean asked, pressing much too close for comfort.

"No, I'm fine," she lied. "But thanks...both of you...for helping." She realized she should say something far more gracious and grateful, but the last thing she wanted to do was encourage either of them. Things would be a lot more pleasant if they decided she was a jerk.

Then, just as her manners were threatening to win out over her better judgment, she noticed Benito was staring at something and followed his gaze downward.

"Sit here for a minute," he said, easing her onto a stair.

She couldn't see anything on the darkly polished floor, but he leaned down and wiped his hand across it, saying, "There's a slippery patch right here at the bottom of the stairs. That's what sent you flying."

Dean dropped to his haunches to check.

"It's some sort of oil," Benito said, examining his hand.

Dean rubbed his fist across the spot a few times, cleaning up whatever was there. "Floor polish, maybe?" he suggested, standing up and wiping his hand on his jeans.

"Uh-uh," Benito said. "Doesn't smell like it." He put his finger to his mouth. "It's salad oil...no, mayonnaise, maybe."

"My special mayonnaise," Zoe said.

Benito glanced a question at her.

"Well, actually it's Chicken's special mayonnaise. But he knows I love it, so he made a gallon of it after I arrived."

"That doesn't explain why there was some on the floor," Benito said. A disturbing question had formed in his mind—about whether Zoe's accidental fall had really been an accident.

"The crew are always making themselves snacks," she said. "So someone probably just put too much mayo in a sandwich. If he was walking and eating at the same time, a bit could have squished out and hit the floor."

Benito rubbed his jaw thoughtfully. That sounded like a reasonable explanation. Of course, it had looked as if a lot more than a *bit* had hit the floor, but he was so damned worried about what El Gato might be up to that anything even slightly suspicious was enough to start his mind revving.

Absently, he began collecting Zoe's scattered drawings. The thought of El Gato, or anyone else for that matter, coming up with the idea of spreading mayo on the floor...it didn't really make much sense. And the thought of anyone intentionally targeting Zoe made no sense at all. She must have just arrived in the wrong place at the wrong time.

He picked up the last of the sketches and turned back to her. "Zoe, you might have a minor concussion. Why don't you go and lie down for a while."

She hesitated, then said, "Actually, I *have* ended up with a headache. Maybe I'll just stretch out on a deck chair for a few minutes. Get a little air."

"Good idea," Cooper said. "I'll go up with you. You shouldn't be alone until you're sure you're all right."

"No, no," she told him quickly. "Thanks, but I'm fine. It's a very little headache."

"Okay if I hang on to these sketches for the moment?" Benito said. "I'd like to have a look at them."

Zoe began to nod, then quickly stopped. Without another word, she started up the stairs, firmly clutching the handrail.

Benito glanced at Cooper, not liking the way he was following her with his eyes and liking the leer on his face even less. For some reason, the thought of Cooper having the hots for Zoe bugged the hell out of him.

BENITO GAVE ZOE time to get settled on deck, then wandered up to see her father, unable to shake the nagging suspicion that someone had been meant to slip on that damned mayo and crack their head open.

But even if that were true, he still couldn't make any sense of the idea that Zoe was supposed to have been the victim. So maybe it would be best not to say anything about the incident to Mac. With him already concerned about her, it wouldn't take much to make him call off their deal.

From the bridge, the *Yankee Doodle*'s few deck chairs were easily visible, and sure enough, Zoe was in full view, lying peacefully on one of them and looking just fine. So there was no point in getting her father upset.

"What's happening?" Mac asked, looking up from the charts he'd been poring over.

"Nothing much. Just thought I'd mention that I want to go down with the divers."

Mac grinned and asked if he wasn't worried about being shark bait. "Always throngs of reef sharks foraging in shallow water like this, Ben."

He tried to match the captain's grin, but figured he looked entirely as unsettled as the thought of being a shark's lunch made him feel.

"They won't actually give you a problem," Mac said. "Not unless you do something stupid like cut yourself shaving before going down. But look, how about if you dive whenever Zoe does? I'd feel better if you were keeping an eye on her underwater, too."

"No, Mac, that's not exactly what I meant. I want to go down when you have time to keep an eye on Zoe yourself. I'd like to check out those guys you've got coming aboard from Cozumel—make sure everything looks okay to me."

"You mean, make sure one of them isn't your Cat in disguise? That's not possible, Ben. All five of them are expert divers. Marco and I would know right away if someone didn't have years of experience."

Benito nodded, saying, "That's what I figured. And hearing you say it makes me feel better. But it doesn't mean El Gato couldn't be paying one of them to spy."

"Oh." Mac frowned. "Well, I was planning to go down again this afternoon, but—"

"I don't have to dive today, Mac. El Gato won't make a move until after you've started raising the treasure."

"Yeah," the captain said, looking down at his daughter. Obviously, he couldn't think about El Gato without worrying about her. "Zoe show you and Cooper those sketches?" he asked, turning back.

"Ahh…we didn't exactly get to looking at them yet, but I've got them here. Thought if you went over them with me, she wouldn't realize how little I know about all this."

"She's going to catch on pretty fast, Ben. You're no expert and she's no dummy."

"Well, let's just try to postpone the inevitable, huh? Like I said yesterday, the more people who know who I am, the more chance of my cover getting blown entirely."

Mac shrugged. "I'll keep my mouth shut. And look, when Zoe does get suspicious, I'll do my best to try and head her offtrack for you. But for now, give me those sketches and we'll go over them."

He spread them out, then began tracing a line on one of his charts. "See," he said, his finger moving across the Gulf of Mexico, "the fleet the *Grifon* was part of started off here, from Veracruz. It crossed the gulf, made it into the Caribbean, then the hurricane caught it. But the *Grifon* was way back, bringing up the rear, and she made a run for it, looking for shelter."

"So," Benito said, pointing to the little red tag indicating where the *Yankee Doodle* was anchored, "you're searching here on the assumption the captain thought he'd find shelter between the mainland and Isla Cozumel."

"Right. Three ships in the fleet survived the storm. When Zoe was doing her thesis research in Seville, she came across an obscure report written by one of the surviving captains. It made her virtually certain the *Grifon* sank in here. The storm would have slammed her into the shallow reefs off the island and wrecked her, then the water would have carried her onto the shoals.

"So what Zoe's sketches show," Mac went on, turning his attention to them, "is approximately where the *Grifon* would have ended up. See, the artifacts we found had been swept away from the main wreck, but both Zoe's calculations and our sonar readings say the *Grifon* should be somewhere right beneath us.''

"Buried in that twenty feet of sifting sand you mentioned this morning."

"Right. Kind of like the needle in the haystack, Ben. Only this needle is worth fifty million bucks. See this little sweep of marks here?''

"Uh-huh.''

''Well, that's her best guess as to what Cooper was asking about—how spread out the treasure's likely to be.''

Benito stared at the formulas and numbers Zoe had scribbled along the sides of the sketches and shook his head. ''I get the general idea, but as far as how she figured it out goes . . .''

"Look,'' Mac said, shuffling the sketches back into a pile. ''With Zoe right down there under my nose, why don't you take these away and study them? That'll make things clearer.''

''Yeah, maybe it would help,'' he agreed, picking them up.

He gazed at the top one for a minute, the sinking feeling in his stomach telling him that spending a month of Sundays looking at them wouldn't help him make sense of all those numbers. If Zoe dragged him into a discussion about the fine points of her calculations, his cover would be blown in five seconds flat.

IN THE FOGGY STATE between sleep and wakefulness, Zoe could hear the divers putting on their equipment, getting ready for the afternoon dive. Above, gulls were screaming, hopeful the activity on deck had something to do with food.

The sunshine and fresh air had put her to sleep. And had taken care of the headache. But she'd been having the strangest dream.

No, not strange exactly...more like erotic. Yes, that was the word. She'd been dreaming the only erotic dream she'd had in her entire life. And she was darned curious about what would have happened next.

Maybe, if she lay perfectly still and didn't open her eyes, she could recapture it.

There'd been an absolutely gorgeous bronze man who'd looked like one of the gods of ancient Greece.

He had an incredibly broad chest and had been leaning over her, his body practically touching hers, his face so close to hers that she could feel the warmth of his breath on her cheek.

And he'd been caressing her, moving his hands over her body so sensually he'd practically melted her.

Yes, she was getting right back into it now . . . could actually feel his hand resting on her arm.

It was a warm, strong hand. She liked its touch. And she knew that if she could drift back to sleep, he'd begin caressing her again. She smiled . . . then jumped a foot when he said her name.

Her eyes flashed open and she was staring into Benito Cárdenas's face.

He was sitting sideways on the lounge chair beside her and, oh, Lord, *his* hand was on her arm and *he* was leaning over her and she could feel *his* breath on her cheek.

He couldn't possibly have been the man in her dream, though. Erotic and Benito Cárdenas didn't belong in the same dream. At least, not in one of hers.

But...well, he certainly did look a whole lot like that ancient Greek god she'd dreamed up.

She scrambled into a sitting position, the motion making her realize her head was still throbbing. Maybe she actually did have a bit of a concussion. That might explain how she could have had a dream about Mr. Arrogance, that hadn't been a nightmare.

Or maybe... He *had* seemed genuinely concerned when she'd fallen. Maybe she'd been misjudging him somewhat and her subconscious had been—

"Sorry," he said. "Didn't mean to startle you."

The way he was grinning, though, said he thought it was darned funny that he had, and she didn't find it even slightly humorous.

She hadn't misjudged him in the least. Not only was he a jerk, he was a jerk with a warped sense of humor.

She glanced around, wondering if anyone had noticed the way she'd jumped when he spoke. No one seemed to be paying any attention.

Her father was engrossed in a conversation with Marco Vinelli, likely about the new equipment the head diver would be spending the afternoon checking over. And the other divers were all still busy with their scuba tanks.

"I just wanted to return your sketches," Benito said.

She looked back at him coolly, saying, "Thank you. Did you make any sense of them?"

"Uh-huh. Perfect sense. I don't think you have to explain anything."

"I'll take them back to my cabin, then," she told him, reaching for them.

The next instant, Billy Bird zoomed through the air and landed with a shrill screech on the end of Benito's lounger.

"Geez!" he snapped. "Does that damned bird always go around scaring people?"

Zoe barely managed not to laugh. "You should feel honored that he wants to sit with you."

Benito glared at Billy, clearly thinking that was a dubious honor. "What's he got there?" he asked.

She took a closer look and saw that Billy was holding something gold in his big beak.

"Billy," she said, "give that to me."

The parrot cocked his head from one side to the other, then strutted a few steps along the lounger and dropped what he was holding into Benito's lap.

"It's a coin," he muttered, picking it up. "An old coin."

"Oh, Billy," she said, eyeing the bird with annoyance. "Where did you get that?"

"Captain Mac."

"From Daddy's cabin? You took something from Daddy's cabin again?"

The bird nodded his head and she shook hers, saying, "Billy, you know you shouldn't steal things."

"Captain Mac," Billy repeated.

"He's a thief?" Benito said.

"Not exactly a thief. He can open the cabin doors with his feet, though, and Dad leaves all kinds of souvenirs from salvages sitting around. I keep telling him to put the valuable ones away, but he never listens. What did Billy take this time? It's something he shouldn't be playing with, isn't it."

"Ahh…" Benito said, holding it between his thumb and forefinger and staring at it.

"Well?" she pressed. "Is it valuable? Hand struck? Can you see the mint and assayer marks?"

"Ahh..." Benito said again, his voice sounding sort of strangled. "I can't quite make them out."

She took the coin from him and glanced at it, thinking he must have a problem with his vision. The marks were perfectly clear.

"Billy," she said sternly, "you're going to have to stop taking this sort of thing."

"Valuable, huh?" Ben said. "I mean, I realized that much, of course."

Zoe nodded slowly, starting to wonder if the government's expert was quite as knowledgeable as he should be.

"There's an interesting story about the ship this came from," she said. "It was Spanish, but the coin's New World. You realized that much, too, though."

"Of course," he said.

"The ship sank off the Florida Keys and..." She paused, tossing the coin back to him. "About what date would you say this was?"

"Ahh..."

"Just take a rough guess," she prompted, now wondering if he had a speech impediment.

"Oh...seventeen-hundreds sometime, I imagine."

She stared at him for a moment, then recovered enough to smile and say, "Good guess."

He stopped looking as if he were sweating bullets and smiled back at her.

"I just have to speak to Dad for a second," she said, breathing a sigh of relief when she saw he was still talking to Marco. "I'll be right back."

She raced across the deck, her heart pounding, remembering every word of her father's story about a gang of modern-day pirates stealing the treasure Carl Medeiros had raised, then blowing up the *Pegasus*.

And when she'd asked if he was worried that might happen to the *Yankee,* he'd said, "Not really."

But if Benito Cárdenas was an archaeologist, then she was the Queen of Sheba, and her father didn't realize he had an imposter aboard.

She skidded to a stop and stood in polite silence for a few seconds.

"So once you're on the bottom," Marco was saying, "head a hundred yards or so straight off the stern. If you start working away from the ship about there..."

He paused, glancing at Zoe as she edged her way between him and her father. Then he moved aside.

Marco Vinelli was a strong, wiry little guy, about her father's age and with gray hair. But that was where the similarities ended.

The head diver was a good foot shorter than the captain. And Zoe was certain that, when she'd grown taller than Marco, he'd developed a complex about it. Since the summer she'd been fifteen, he'd always tried to avoid standing directly beside her.

She gave him an apologetic smile, then said, "Dad, I have to talk to you."

"Zoe, you can see I'm busy."

"It's important!"

He gave her a look that said it had better be, and dragged her a few feet along the rail.

"All right," he said, stopping and glaring down at her. "What's so almighty important?"

"Dad, I think Benito Cárdenas could be the guy who blew up Carl's ship. And if he is, he's here to try to do the same thing to ours."

Her father stared at her for a moment, then said, "Zoe, you shouldn't have lain in that hot sun for so long."

"No! Really. Billy Bird took something from your cabin again—a gold coin. And I asked Benito what date he thought it was and he said seventeen-hundreds. But anyone who knows basic archaeology, let alone anyone who's an examiner for the archives, knows all New World coins were dated from 1622 on. Dad, Benito Cárdenas is a fake."

"Zoe . . . that just isn't so. Whatever Ben said . . . he probably wasn't thinking. Or maybe he misunderstood what you were asking. Or you misunderstood his answer. Don't worry about it, huh?"

"Don't worry about it? Have you slipped a gear? I'm telling you, Benito Cárdenas isn't legit. What's he doing on our ship?"

"Baby, he *is* legit. You can't take one thing he says—that you probably got confused, anyway—and blow it out of proportion. He had nothing to do with what happened to Carl, and he's not going to do anything here. At least, nothing except look over the artifacts we raise."

She shook her head, knowing something wasn't right. "Dad, why is he even aboard this soon? On every other salvage I've been involved in, we've never had a government type even drop by for months. Not until after we've had half the treasure aboard."

"Well, they've changed the rules this time, Zoe. But look, when I was getting the salvage license, Miguel Lopez gave Ben rave reviews. So let me get back to business and don't worry."

He turned away, took a couple of steps, then stopped and looked back. "And do *not*," he said in his sternest, this-is-the-captain-speaking voice, "go trying that ridiculous idea on anyone else, understand? Don't you say a word about Ben. You'd just get people upset when everything's okay."

She stood watching in disbelief as her father strode back along the deck and resumed his conversation with Marco Vinelli.

That *had* been quite a smack on the head she'd taken earlier. So it was possible she'd gotten confused . . . but she was certain she hadn't.

It was her father who didn't know what was going on. Maybe he'd been diving too deep over the winter. Or spending longer stretches than he should have on the bottom. The pressure could addle a man's brains.

Benito Cárdenas definitely wasn't who he claimed to be. And if the ship's captain didn't intend to find out who the imposter was, she'd darned well have to do it herself.

Chapter Three

The divers started down and her father was strapping on his gear, but Zoe hadn't yet decided what to do. She gazed along the deck to where Benito Cárdenas was sitting with Billy Bird.

The man was definitely a phony. Undoubtedly a crook. And if he *was* the guy who'd blown up Carl's ship, he was also a murderer. Not exactly someone she wanted to tangle with. But to get her father to tangle with him she was going to need evidence.

If there was any clue aboard ship as to Benito's real identity, it would either be on him or in his belongings.

She didn't want even to imagine what she'd have to do to find a clue on him, so she'd start with his belongings. And if she was going to play Mata Hari, now was the time to do it without much risk.

Chicken would be in the galley. Sandy Braukis, the first mate, was standing watch. Marco Vinelli had headed down to the equipment room, and he was such a stickler about the diving gear that checking out the new stuff would keep him busy the entire afternoon.

Besides, Marco, Chicken and Sandy shared one of the two aft cabins. They'd have no business going into the other.

Mentally, she accounted for Benito's cabin mates. Marco's two full-time divers, Sam Johnson and Danny Doyle, would be thirty feet below for the next two or three hours. That left only Dean Cooper and Jake the Rake to worry about.

She glanced at her watch and decided Jake would be cleaning up after lunch for a good half hour yet. And even though she didn't know where their photographer was, none of the crew ever sat around in their quarters during the day. So all she had to do was figure out how to ensure Benito stayed away from the cabin while she searched it.

"*All* you have to do?" she muttered to herself, starting anxiously along the deck and praying for inspiration. She reached Benito, still uninspired, and manufactured a smile.

He didn't produce one in return, just shot a glare in Billy's direction and said, "Your bird doesn't like me. Look what he did to my hand."

She looked at the three long red scratches. Billy had almost drawn blood. He was certainly a big help. If he did that again, Benito would be heading to his cabin for a first-aid kit.

"Sometimes he forgets how sharp his talons are," she said. "But I'll bet he was just trying to be friends."

"Sure," Benito said.

"Friends," Billy said.

Zoe said, "See? I was right."

To prove she had been, Billy flapped up onto Benito's shoulder.

The man didn't say a word, but he looked as if he'd rather have boiling oil poured on him.

"I'll tell you what," Zoe said, inspiration striking at last. "There's something I'd like to talk to you about, but I haven't had lunch yet. Why don't you take Billy and the sketches to my cabin and I'll run down to the galley and grab something. I'll only be a couple of minutes, and you can talk to Billy while you're waiting ... kind of get to know him."

Benito mumbled something under his breath that was undoubtedly insulting to both her and the bird, but she let it pass. Getting into a fight would hardly help convince Benito to go and sit in her cabin so she could rifle through his.

"I'll come down to the galley with you," he said.

"No, that isn't a good idea because ... Chicken doesn't like Billy very much."

"I can't imagine why."

She let that pass, too, saying, "So, I'll see you in a couple of minutes? My cabin's not locked."

For a long moment he looked as if he were going to argue, but finally picked up the sketches and started toward the forward cabins with Billy happily perched on his shoulder.

She checked the observation platform to be sure Sandy wasn't watching her. He wasn't. He was gazing off the starboard side, the sun beating down on his balding head.

It didn't seem many years since his hair had been the gingery blond that had earned him his nickname. Now what was left of it was pure white. Like her father, though, Sandy was still a big, strong man.

Along the deck, Benito and Billy were just about to disappear from sight. The moment they did, she hurried in the opposite direction, slipping through the doorway that led to the tiny passage between the two crew cabins.

She knocked on the one on the port side, just in case. Then, when there was no response, she opened the door.

Benito, she thought, glancing around the claustrophobic space, could hardly have been thrilled when her father booted him out of her cabin and sent him back to the shared quarters.

Not that an imposter deserved any better. In fact, if the *Yankee* had a brig, that would be the appropriate place for Señor Cárdenas. But the crew cabin was far from luxury accommodation.

It housed three lower and three upper berths with barely room to move between them. Six lockers along one wall comprised the total storage space, and the head was tiny. Even so, cabins with their own washrooms were a luxury on salvage ships. Most just had one community head.

A quick check of the lockers' interiors told her which was Benito's. Unlike the others, it was neat and orderly. Successful criminals probably had obsessive personalities. She began rummaging through his clothes, not knowing what she was looking for but hoping that...

She froze at the sound of footsteps outside the cabin, then dived for the head and shoved the door shut.

An instant later she decided hiding wasn't the best idea—especially in a stuffy little washroom.

It had to be either Jake or Dean Cooper coming in, and whoever it was would probably find her. So she'd be smarter to say straight off that she'd had a sudden need and this had been the closest head.

Maybe it was pretty thin, but there wasn't much they could do about it. After all, she *was* the captain's daughter. She started to open the door again, ready to brazen her story out.

Then a man stepped into the cabin.

He wasn't Jake the Rake. And he wasn't Dean Cooper. He was someone who had no business coming in here.

She pressed herself behind the head's door and tried not to breathe. She'd just hide where she was until he left.

ZOE'S CABIN DOOR was partly open, and she eased closer to it, not sure Benito would still be waiting inside for her. But when she peeked in, there he was.

He looked, she thought, stealing quickly across to her father's cabin, thoroughly ticked off. She'd had to hide out in that head for so long he must think she'd taken the time to eat a nine-course lunch.

Quietly, she opened her father's door, hurried over to his desk, and rummaged around in the drawer, looking under the mess of papers for his Colt.

Her hand touched metal, but when she pulled out the gun it was one she hadn't seen before...some kind of little snub-nosed thing she didn't know how to use.

Uneasily, she put it back and kept checking, relieved when she found the Colt was still there, as well. She slipped it from the drawer and checked that the cylinder was full, all the while trying to ignore the way her hands were shaking.

Learning she wasn't the only one suspicious of Benito had made her absolutely certain she hadn't gotten confused during their conversation about the coin. Whoever he really was, Benito Cárdenas was up to no good. And one look at the disaster area Marco Vinelli had turned Benito's locker into would make him realize someone was on to him.

She would have searched through his things neatly, so he wouldn't have known anyone had been in there. But the way Marco had ransacked everything, Benito would have to be blind not to notice.

Pulling her shirt loose from her shorts, she stuck the Colt's cold steel barrel into the back of her waistband, grateful that life aboard a salvage ship had taught her a few things the average archaeologist didn't know.

Then she crossed back from the captain's cabin to her own and stopped outside the partially open door, afraid to confront Benito but not seeing that she had any choice.

Whatever was happening would probably come to a climax the minute he saw his locker. And since she didn't know what he'd do then, she had to try to get the truth out of him before he could do anything.

No, not try to get. She was *going* to get the truth. After all, she was the one with the gun. And as if that weren't enough, Billy Bird was in her cabin. If Benito tried anything, he'd get the surprise of his life.

The thought of what Billy could do tempted her to smile, but when she opened the door more fully the temptation vanished. Next to her berth, Billy's brass perch sat empty.

Benito was standing in front of the window, looking over at her, but the bird was nowhere in sight.

"Where's Billy?" she said, certain she sounded about as casual as if she'd walked in and found someone pointing a machine gun at her.

"Decided he didn't like my company."

"Oh." She pushed the door open even wider, stepped inside and stood watching Benito anxiously.

Those indecent denim cutoffs of his did nothing to conceal the fact that his legs were very, very muscular. And his tank top only emphasized his broad shoulders and the muscles in his chest.

Over the years, her father had taught her a lot about taking care of herself, but Benito Cárdenas was clearly no cream puff. If she tried socking him on that chiseled granite jaw of his, she'd probably break her hand.

Even though she could feel the Colt snugged against the small of her back, this confrontation no longer seemed like a good idea at all.

"You wanted to talk," he said.

She nodded. She had the gun and the cabin door was open. If she screamed or fired, someone would hear and come running.

"You're not..." The words were mere squeaks, so she swallowed hard, then all in one rush said, "You're not an examiner with the archives, so what are you doing aboard the *Yankee*?"

Even as she was asking the question, Benito shot across the cabin, shoved the door closed and leaned against it, blocking her escape.

Terrified, she reached for the Colt. He lunged forward, yanking the gun away from her, knocked her onto her berth and covered her mouth with his hand.

When she tried to struggle he pinned her firmly against the mattress with his body. She couldn't move and couldn't breathe.

"Listen to me!" he whispered fiercely. "I'm not going to hurt you. I'm a federal agent."

What he'd said took a second to sink in. When it did, she realized that if she weren't petrified she'd laugh. Did he take her for a fool?

"Do you understand?" he demanded.

Her brain kicked into overdrive and she nodded. Her best chance had to be to play along with him.

"All right," he said. "Can I trust you to keep quiet if I let you up?"

She nodded again. He was the one with the gun now.

Tentatively, he eased himself off her and sat up, keeping a tight hold of her right wrist.

"A federal agent?" she said, amazed that her voice sounded almost normal when her heart was racing a mile a minute. "You're saying you're FBI?"

"Uh-uh, but similar. The Mexican Policia Federale." He put the Colt behind him on the berth, then fumbled in his back pocket, produced a worn leather case and flipped it open.

A seed of uncertainty began germinating as she stared at the ID. It looked authentic. If he were a serious crook, though, he could have an authentic-looking fake one.

On the other hand, if he were a murderer wouldn't he have done her in the second he realized she was wise to him?

She took a deep breath that didn't calm her half as much as she'd hoped it would, and gazed at him. He didn't look as if he intended to kill her. But then, she'd never knowingly stared a killer in the eye, so how could she be sure what one looked like?

"And when were you planning on telling my father who you really are?" she said.

"He knows. He's the only one aboard who does."

Zoe tried not to look skeptical but was certain she wasn't succeeding.

"When you were getting that gun," he said, nodding toward the Colt, "did you find an automatic in your father's desk?"

She nodded uncertainly.

"Well, that was mine. We didn't think it was a good idea for me to keep it with my things in the crew quarters. You see, Zoe, I'm on board because your father is helping me try to catch the guy who blew up the *Pegasus*. I think he's going to come after the *Grifon*'s treasure."

For half a second she wondered if that could be the truth, then decided it couldn't. Because if Benito Cárdenas were really with the *federales*, if her father had actually agreed to help with some scheme they'd cooked up, Mac would certainly have told her. But if it wasn't the truth, then how did Benito know about that gun in her father's desk?

"Talk to Mac when he's finished diving," Benito was saying. "He'll explain how he got involved."

Benito eyed her for a minute, then slowly released her wrist. She sat rubbing it while she considered making a grab for the Colt. But she didn't have a hope in hell of getting it, so she shifted her attention back to Benito.

A logical little voice in her head was saying that he was for real. Because if he wasn't, he'd have been pretty stupid to make up a lie that she could check with her father. And she had a feeling the last thing Benito Cárdenas was was stupid.

So if he was a *federale* . . . she'd better tell him what had happened in his cabin. Maybe *he'd* know why Marco Vinelli had been rummaging through that locker.

She'd been in the crew cabin because she'd realized Benito wasn't an archaeologist. But why the hell had Marco been there? What had he been looking for?

"Benito . . . ?" she began.

"Uh-huh?"

"Ahh . . . nothing. Figured it out myself."

He looked at her expectantly, but she didn't offer an explanation. A quick second thought told her she'd better hold off saying anything about Marco until she was absolutely certain what was what—certain that somehow, someway, Benito hadn't simply sucked her father in.

Mentally, she began adding up things that had seemed strange earlier. The way her father had so very emphatically insisted she was wrong about Benito's being a crook. Then the way he'd ordered her not to breathe a word about her suspicion.

And if the two of them *were* expecting some dangerous character to show, it would explain why her father hadn't wanted her aboard ship.

It would also, she thought, her internal thermostat notching up and starting a slow, angry burn, mean her father had intentionally been keeping her in the dark—as if she were a child who couldn't be trusted with the truth.

That had to be it, she concluded angrily. Something exciting was going down and these two macho men had been trying to keep her out of it. Her own father, along with Mr. Arrogance here, had decided she wasn't up to being part of whatever plot they'd hatched.

Well, if that's the way they wanted to play, maybe she wouldn't tell Benito about Marco at all. Maybe she'd darned well let Señor Cárdenas figure out for himself who'd searched through his things.

"This guy we're after," he said, "we know him as El Gato. I've been trying to get him for almost three years, Zoe, and I think we've got a good chance of nailing him this time. But if you say anything about who I really am, you'll blow the operation."

"*I'll* blow it?" she snapped. "How about *you'll* blow it—merely by opening your mouth?" She realized how steamed she was but didn't care. The idea of her father and this man . . . damn, but that made her blood boil.

"Do you think the crew are a bunch of cretins?" she demanded. "They've been raising treasure for years, and they know a whole hell of a lot about what they're bringing up. And you won't recognize silver bars from ballast. How did you think you were going to pass yourself off as an expert once we located the wreck?"

"Ahh . . . well, Mac and I figured he could kind of feed me information as we went along. Then, after you'd arrived, well, he told me we wouldn't be able to keep the truth from you for very long, so I assumed that once you knew it you'd give me a hand and—"

"*I'd* give you a hand? Why the hell should I give you a hand when you didn't even tell me what was going on? And my own father! Treating me like I was still thirteen. I'm going to strangle him for this."

"Zoe, the only reason he didn't level with you was because I asked him not to."

"That isn't the point! The point is that he went along with you instead of...oh, damn. I have to talk to him. Right now." She pushed herself off the berth and started across the cabin.

Benito grabbed her wrist again, saying, "Zoe, he's down with the divers."

"I know where he is! I'm not an idiot—despite what you both apparently think. I'm going down to get him."

"Oh? Well, if you're not an idiot, then why the hell are you talking about diving only hours after you fell on your head? I already told you that you might have a concussion."

She gritted her teeth until the urge to suggest what he should do with his medical opinion passed, then said, "If you wouldn't mind letting go of me and getting out of my cabin, I'd like to change—so I can go down and get my father."

Benito shot daggers at her with his dark eyes but released his grip. "Just don't talk to Mac where anyone can overhear."

She glared a few daggers of her own while he backed out of the cabin. He really must think she was an idiot.

He closed the door, and she grabbed a bathing suit from the wardrobe, pulled a quick change act, then headed to the equipment room for a tank.

BENITO PACED ANGRILY PAST the open gate again, hoping to hell Zoe was the type who cooled off as fast as she heated up. If she laced into Mac while she was still mad as a hornet, everyone aboard ship would probably hear them.

But maybe she'd already gotten over her tantrum. Maybe she'd changed her mind about going down to get her father and would just wait until he came up.

Those hopeful maybes were good for about three seconds. Then Zoe stomped out onto the deck, toting diving gear, and began marching over to the gate.

She was wearing a dark blue bathing suit that almost made him forget he was furious with her. It definitely made him aware he hadn't seen her dressed in so little before . . . and very aware of the way she filled that suit. And then there were those gorgeous long legs he kept noticing . . .

He turned away from her and firmly told himself this was neither the time nor the place. Nor the woman. No, above all, not the woman.

It was one thing to be reminded his hormones were still in working order, but he liked more positive attributes in a woman than just good looks. And Zoe MacLeish was a hot-tempered, headstrong pain-in-the-butt who was liable to sink him.

He glanced at her again, considering having another go at talking sense to her, but she'd apparently decided to pretend he was the invisible man.

Wordlessly, without even looking at him, she shrugged into her tank and slipped on her mask.

Totally unreasonable. That was clearly one of her main problems. Only a totally unreasonable person would go down and interrupt her father the way she was about to. And nobody could talk sense to a woman like that.

She checked the air line, then adjusted her weight belt and started down the ladder, leaving him gazing after her and swearing to himself.

When she reached the water, she put on her fins, glanced up for half a second, then sank beneath the surface so smoothly there wasn't the slightest sound to interrupt the rhythmic lapping of waves against the *Yankee*'s hull.

For a moment, her long dark hair trailed on the surface. As it vanished, Benito headed for the crew cabin.

He'd only walked a few feet when he heard a splash and looked down at the water again.

All he saw was a series of circles just off the ladder, rippling away from their centers as if someone had tossed something into the sea.

But the only person in sight was the first mate, Sandy Braukis. And he was standing watch up on the observation platform, looking in the opposite direction.

Benito started off once more. A moment later a shout split the air and froze him in his tracks.

"Shark!" Sandy was screaming. "Shark!"

Wheeling to the rail, Benito stared down. He couldn't see a thing. Unless that dark, moving shadow...

A second later Zoe's head appeared above the water, about ten yards from the ship. She was shoving up her mask when another shape broke the surface.

His heart stood still. The dorsal fin of a shark was slicing through the sea and the dark shadow had become an ominous shape—a sleek body that looked like a live torpedo.

Suddenly he was staring at a scene from *Jaws*. The shark wasn't more than fifteen feet from Zoe and was slowly circling her. Zoe was the sole focus of that eating machine's attention.

He kicked off his sneakers, adrenaline pumping like mad, his eyes frantically searching for a weapon.

Sandy was yelling and pointing down at a wooden chest on the deck.

Benito raced over to it and threw open the lid. Inside were a few coiled ropes, a couple of life jackets. And a spear gun. A big-game spear gun with a detonating head. He grabbed the gun and tore across to the gate.

The ladder reached far beneath the waterline, and he kept climbing down until only his head and shoulders were above the surface.

That was as far as he could go. He needed the ladder for support. He'd never be able to aim accurately while swimming, and he couldn't take a chance on hitting Zoe.

He gazed anxiously across the water, his heart thudding. The shark was still about fifteen feet from her, still swimming in slow, lazy circles around her.

She'd taken off her scuba tank and was holding it in front of her while she treaded water. He doubted it would be enough protection if that shark made a move. Her terrified expression said she didn't believe it would be, either.

He had to think, had to figure out what to do when he didn't know much more about sharks than he did about sunken treasure. What he did know was that if a shark decided to attack it would strike like lightning. The knowledge did nothing to reassure him.

"Zoe," he called, not certain she realized he was there. "Zoe, I've got a gun. You're going to be all right."

Her gaze flickered to him for a second, then she went back to watching the shark.

Benito leveled the gun as far as he could below the surface, disengaged the safety and aimed at the shark. He cocked the gun but didn't shoot. His only chance for that would be when it circled to the side, when Zoe wasn't in the line of fire. And even then . . .

He was a crack shot on land, but he'd only used a spear gun a couple of times. And that shark was a good six-footer. Looking at its long shape made him feel as if he'd be trying to kill Moby Dick with a blow dart.

Aim for its brain, he silently told himself. *If it comes to the crunch, aim for its brain.* Hitting it there would assure an instant kill.

But aiming and hitting were two different things. And Mac had said there were always throngs of sharks foraging in these shallow waters. If he shot this one, the blood would instantly attract more, so shooting had to be his last resort.

"Zoe," he called again. "Start moving toward the ship. Stay to one side. Don't get in my sight line."

She didn't answer, but began to inch her way closer, her eyes never leaving the shark.

It continued circling, its fin cutting a smooth line through the water each time it passed between them. Gradually, as Zoe drew nearer to the ship, it stopped circling and began swimming parallel to the *Yankee*'s hull—back and forth in a line behind her.

Benito kept the gun trained three feet in front of that fin, where the beast's head would be, and kept his finger on the trigger, not daring to even blink.

But finally, when Zoe was only about two yards from the hull, the shark turned and headed away.

He felt an incredible rush of relief. Then, in the split second before he reached out a hand to Zoe, that fin sliced around in the water and the shark raced directly at them.

He shot the spear. And the instant zoomed into fast forward and slow motion at the same time.

The shark was so close he could see every detail through the clear water—its savage jaws agape, dagger-sharp teeth exposed, its eyes rolling back.

Then the spear drove into its head and the water around them became a wash of red.

Benito dropped the gun and grabbed Zoe's arm, not knowing whether the shark was dead or merely wounded. But for the moment they had a chance. He pulled Zoe onto the ladder and shoved her up ahead of him.

They reached the top and Sandy Braukis hauled them aboard—babbling nonstop about how he'd thought they were goners.

Zoe collapsed to her knees, trying to free her tank strap. Benito clung to the rail, not certain his legs would support him, gradually growing aware of a commotion below.

He looked down and whispered, "Good God."

The water was alive with a feeding frenzy of sharks, and they were still coming from all directions, racing for a piece of their dead mate. There had to be fifty thrashing brutes, fighting over the meat.

Sandy said, "Thank God the divers aren't working directly beneath the ship. They're far enough away to be safe."

Then Zoe made a funny little noise and Benito turned to her. She was sitting by the open gate and staring down at the scene, her entire body shaking.

He knelt beside her, wrapped his arms around her, drawing her close.

She pressed her face against his chest, murmuring, "That was almost us . . . that was almost us."

"But it wasn't, Zoe," he whispered into her wet hair. "It wasn't. We're okay."

She clung to him for another minute, then drew back a little and gave him a tremulous smile, saying, "I owe you a major thanks."

"De nada," he murmured.

She eased away from him, but her expression was still saying "thank you."

He sat watching her for a moment, his gaze caught in the depths of her green eyes.

Right here and now, he was having a lot of trouble remembering that she was a hot-tempered pain-in-the-butt. Right here and now, she was a woman in serious need of reassurance. And hell, what would it hurt him to give it to her?

He was moving to put his arms around her again and to tell her that everything really was all right when Sandy spoke.

"Zoe?" he said. "Zoe, what did you do wrong?"

Benito glanced up at the first mate's weathered face. "What do you mean, wrong?"

"I'm fifty years old," Sandy said slowly, "and I've never seen anything quite like that before. All the stories you hear about sharks attacking people are a bunch of garbage. It only happens if there's blood in the water. Or if a person's hurt, sharks can sense it. But there was nothing like that, so Zoe must have done something to attract that one."

"Zoe?" Benito said, turning back to her.

She'd started quietly crying. Obviously, the last thing she needed was someone telling her she'd been at fault.

Tentatively, he took her hands in his. "Zoe? Zoe, listen. If you did something wrong it's okay. Everybody makes mistakes and—"

"No," she said. "It wasn't me. I..." She swallowed hard, then went on. "Someone threw something off the ship. Just after I started my dive."

"I didn't see anyone on deck," Sandy said. "Except for the two of you."

"I didn't, either," Benito told him. "But I heard something hit the water. And when I looked down I could see the ripples it made."

Zoe swallowed again, then said, "I saw it sinking past me. Lord, it passed by so close I could have touched it. Then all at once the shark was there, devouring it and...and that's what set him off."

"But what was it?" Benito said.

She slowly shook her head, as if she couldn't quite believe what she was about to say. "It was meat, Benito. Someone threw a huge chunk of raw meat overboard."

Chapter Four

Zoe had managed to stop trembling, but only on the outside. Now she stood leaning against the rail and waited for either Benito or Sandy to say something.

That meat hadn't fallen from the sky. Someone on the *Yankee* had pitched it, and she desperately wanted to hear an explanation—other than the obvious one.

Finally, Sandy said, "It had to be an accident."

She nodded encouragement for him to continue. That wasn't much of an explanation so far, but maybe it got better.

"I guess," he went on, "whoever threw it overboard didn't realize you were diving and—"

"Sure," Benito snapped. "People always go around casually tossing chunks of raw meat into shark-infested waters."

Sandy gave him a glare. "Well, what the hell do you figure, Cárdenas? That someone was deliberately trying to...to scare Zoe?"

Oh, Lord. Sandy had caught himself, but she knew he'd been going to say, trying to *kill* Zoe. And that was exactly the obvious line of thinking she didn't want to hear.

"What I figure," Benito was saying, "is the odds it was deliberate are damned high."

She swallowed hard. Benito didn't believe it was an accident any more than Sandy did, so why was she trying to fool herself? Someone wanted her dead.

"We'd better question everyone on board," Benito said. "Find out who was responsible and if he has any kind of believable explanation. Look, I'll head down to—"

"Not so fast," Sandy interrupted. "You aren't running the show. When Mac's not around, I'm in charge. I'll decide what we're going to do."

Benito looked as if what *he* was going to do was take a poke at Sandy, so Zoe quickly said, "Sandy's right, Benito. When the captain's not aboard the first mate's in charge. But Sandy, I do think we should talk to everyone, shouldn't we? I mean, I really want to get to the bottom of this."

"Me, too," Benito said.

"Yeah," Sandy muttered. "Yeah, we'd better get right on it. Okay, let's see. We should start with Chicken and Jake. They're the only ones who would have had any possible reason to be walking around with a chunk of meat. And who else is aboard?"

"Marco," Zoe said.

Marco. Her mind had been so focused on that shark almost eating her that she'd forgotten about what had happened earlier. But saying Marco's name reminded her.

Could his going into the crew cabin and searching through Benito's locker possibly be connected to the shark episode?

What if Marco had realized she was hiding in that head, watching him? What if he'd been trying to shut her up about it . . . permanently?

No, no, no! That couldn't be it. Her imagination was just running riot. In the future, she'd better not read so many murder mysteries. And at the moment, she'd better tell Benito about Marco checking out that locker.

"And Dean Cooper," Sandy said.

She glanced along the deck. The photographer had appeared at the far end and was walking toward them.

"Everyone else is diving," Sandy added quietly. "So we've got four possibilities."

While they stood watching Dean approach, Benito leaned close to Zoe's ear and murmured, "Five possibilities. That meat could have been tossed from the observation platform. We can't rule out Sandy."

"Of course we can," she whispered fiercely. The idea of its being the first mate was inconceivable.

"It could have been *anyone* aboard ship," Benito insisted.

Zoe stared at him, her thoughts whirling. *Anyone aboard ship* included him. And the ID he'd shown her hadn't entirely convinced her he was for real.

What if he wasn't, after all? What if he was the one who'd thrown that meat, then saved her life as part of some crazy scheme to make her trust him?

She glanced out over the sea, desperately wanting to talk to her father. But in shallow water, with almost no limit on bottom time, the divers always took down enough spare air tanks to let them search for hours. And here she was, aboard ship with someone who'd tried to kill her.

It didn't take much rational thought to realize it couldn't have been Benito, though. He'd been standing right by the gate when she'd gone down. And when she'd glanced up from the bottom of the ladder, he'd still been watching her. And he definitely hadn't been holding a chunk of meat.

So maybe he was the one person she could trust—ironic as it might be that he was also the man she'd recently suspected of being a murderer.

"Zoe," he murmured, his dark eyes holding her gaze, "until we get some answers, think carefully before you say anything."

Think carefully. All right, that made sense. She'd be wise to set aside the issue of Marco's search-and-destroy mission for the moment. Telling Benito what had happened, while anyone else was around, wasn't a good idea.

Uneasily, she stared at Sandy's broad back. He'd been aware she was diving, so if he'd wanted to...but he'd never harm her. No more than Marco would.

Only she couldn't imagine that Chicken...she'd known the cook her entire life. And Jake the Rake liked her. She was sure he did. And Dean...with those hungry eyes of his, there were undoubtedly things he'd like to do to her, but she doubted killing her was one of them.

There just *had* to be some explanation.

"*Qué pasa,* folks?" Dean said, joining them.

"Where've you been, Cooper?" Sandy demanded. "For the past twenty minutes or so."

"What? I miss something?"

"Just answer the question."

Dean shrugged and said he'd been in the strong room since lunch. "I had to take one of my cameras apart, and the table in there's good to work on."

"Where's the camera now?" Benito said.

Dean looked at the three of them in turn, obviously waiting for someone to clue him in.

When no one did, he shrugged again, saying, "It's still on the table. In pieces. I'm just out stretching my legs."

"Well, something's come up," Sandy said. "I need you to stand watch now."

"Sure. I'll just go finish with the camera, then—"

"*Right* now," Sandy snapped.

"Yeah . . . yeah, sure. Right now." He waited for a moment, still clearly hoping to hear what was going on, then gave up and started off for the observation platform.

"That takes care of one possibility," Sandy said.

"Maybe we should wander by the strong room," Benito suggested. "Just make sure there *is* a camera in it."

Sandy looked annoyed that he hadn't thought of the idea himself, but nodded. "Yeah, maybe we should."

They headed inside and checked. Once the *Grifon* was located and there was raised treasure stored inside the strong room, it would be securely locked. But at the moment, nobody bothered locking it any more than they did the cabins.

It stood open and empty, except for the parts of Dean's camera that were spread out on the table.

"Like I said," Sandy muttered, "that takes care of one possibility. So let's go see what Chicken and Jake have to say for themselves."

They'd barely started along a passageway that led to the aft stairs when they ran into Marco. Zoe's stomach muscles tightened.

While Sandy asked the head diver where he'd been, she told herself she was being ridiculous.

"Equipment room," Marco said. "Haven't set foot out of it since the divers went down after lunch."

Anxiously, she bit her lip, knowing that was a lie. Maybe the time had come to say something... or maybe not.

She glanced at Benito, but he'd already started off with Sandy again.

"Something wrong, Zoe?" Marco said.

"No," she managed, forcing a smile. "No, nothing's wrong at all. Just going to the galley," she added, easing past him and ordering herself not to break into a run.

By the time she caught up with the others, they were halfway down the staircase. She took it carefully, remembering what had happened earlier.

On the far side of the dining area, the galley door was open. Both Chicken and Jake were inside.

Sandy didn't waste a second getting to the point. "Somebody threw a hunk of meat overboard. What do you two know about it?"

Chicken wheeled toward Jake and wordlessly accused him.

"It wasn't me," he said, shaking his head so hard his greasy dark hair whipped from side to side.

Zoe eyed them closely—short, skinny, bald Chicken staring up at his tall, skinny, long-haired assistant. Neither of their expressions told her a darned thing.

"Well, it sure as hell wasn't me," Chicken snapped. "Dammit, Jake, when I told you to get rid of it I didn't mean overboard. Your brain slip to your butt, boy?''

"It wasn't me," Jake protested more loudly. "I know better."

"You told Jake to get rid of a chunk of meat, though," Benito said to Chicken.

"Yeah. There's a butcher on Cozumel who won't be gettin' no more of the *Yankee*'s money. Durned roast was bad. So I left it on the counter and told Jake to take care of it. But I meant he should wrap it up for the garbage."

"I knew what you meant," Jake snapped. "But two seconds later you sent me off to get stuff from storage, remember? And when I got back, you were gone and so was the meat. So I figured you took care of it yourself."

"You went somewhere while Jake was gone, Chicken?" Benito asked.

Chicken glanced at him. "Yeah, I went somewhere. Nature calls, y'know. What about it?"

"What about it," Sandy said, "is that the meat hit the water right where Zoe was diving. And she had a shark for company in about two seconds."

"Holy..." Chicken muttered, his eyes flashing to her. "You okay, honey?"

She nodded. Chicken's wizened face was full of concern. She'd known it couldn't have been him.

Jake, though, looked decidedly...just exactly how did he look? She wasn't sure if he seemed concerned or guilty. She needed a course in body language.

"So..." Benito said, "...the meat was just sitting on the counter while you were both gone. How long ago would that have been?''

"Maybe I was gone one or three quarters of an hour," Jake told him.

"And anyone could have wandered in and taken it," Benito concluded.

"Who in tarnation," Chicken said, "would take a hunk of rotten meat?"

That, Benito thought, was the million-dollar question. The mayo this morning might have been an accident. But two 'accidents' in rapid succession? Hell, at this point he wouldn't bet a single peso on either incident having been accidental.

So what in God's name was going on here? He'd come aboard to trap El Gato, and he knew damned well that the mysterious criminal wasn't, in reality, one of Mac's permanent crew.

Even though that possibility had been incredibly unlikely, he'd checked it out. And in the past year, while the mastermind had been pulling off crimes in Mexico, every one of the *Yankee*'s present crew were on that salvage operation in South America. Not even El Gato could be in two places at once.

Of course, one of the crew could be working for him. He'd enlisted insiders' help before. But how in hell would killing Zoe fit into whatever plan the crook might have dreamed up this time?

He glanced at her, thinking that was a question deserving serious consideration.

Zoe was taking long, deep breaths, obviously trying to relax. She must have been hoping against hope that somebody would have an explanation for what had happened.

Not one of them was admitting to knowing a thing. But one of them was lying.

BILLY BIRD STRUTTED a few steps along his brass perch and flapped his wings at Benito, saying, ''Don't yell. Don't yell.''

Benito shot a *drop dead* glance at the bird, but Zoe kept her eyes glued to the man. He had more gall than ten men put together.

He might have saved her life and she might be darned grateful. But surely even that didn't oblige her to put up with his blasted know-it-all arrogance. In her own cabin, yet.

Benito turned his attention back to Zoe, no longer having the slightest bit of trouble remembering that she was a hot-tempered pain-in-the-butt.

Without a doubt, she was the most infuriating woman he'd ever met. The minute he'd told her who he really was she should have filled him in about his locker being searched.

''Don't yell,'' Billy muttered again.

That probably was good advice, but Benito was so damned mad he wasn't sure he could follow it. ''I don't know what Marco was looking for, either,'' he said, unable to keep anger out of his voice. ''But I damn well *do* know you should have mentioned his little search.''

''And precisely when should I have told you?'' Zoe snapped. ''When I thought you were a criminal? Or once you'd shown me that ID I figured could be fake? Or in front of Sandy and Dean? Or in the galley? Or maybe when I found out you and my father had been keeping major secrets from me. Dammit, the minute he comes up I'm going to straighten him out.''

"What the hell are you two up to in here?" Mac shouted, bursting into the cabin. "You're coming through loud and clear in the passageway."

"Captain Mac!" Billy screeched. "Captain Mac!"

"Shut up, Billy," Mac ordered, shoving the door closed and looking from Benito to Zoe.

The captain's hair was wet, and drops of water glistened on his skin. The afternoon dive had obviously just ended.

Zoe had transferred her glare to her father, and Benito knew exactly where she was heading with that temper of hers. Before she could get going, he said, "Cool it, Zoe. You can argue with Mac all you want later. First, we have to tell him what's been going on."

She gave him a look of pure fury that almost made him wish he'd let the shark have her. Then she crossed her arms and leaned against the wall without saying another word.

"Okay," Mac said, "what's been going on?"

Quickly, Benito began filling him in. Hearing that Zoe had gone to look through Benito's things made the captain grin.

"Warned you we couldn't fool her for long, Ben," he said.

"There's more," Benito told him, not grinning back. "A lot more."

When he got to the part about Marco Vinelli pulling his search routine, Mac started to look puzzled. "What the hell was he looking for?"

"I don't know," Benito said. "But it made Zoe confront me about who I was, and I had to fill her in on what's going on. About El Gato and—"

"I want to talk to you about that, Dad," Zoe interrupted. "Why didn't you tell me Benito was a *federale?* And that this El Gato character's likely to appear? I'm not a child, you know."

"Zoe!" Benito snapped. "Give it a rest, huh?"

She shot him another furious look and Billy muttered, "Don't yell. Don't yell."

Benito ignored both of them and plunged into the story about the shark. That one made Mac lose three shades of his tan.

"Good God," he said, gazing at Zoe as if he were in shock. "You sure you're okay, baby?"

When she nodded, he slowly shook his head, saying, "I can't believe anyone would try to kill you. It must have been an accident. But why didn't whoever did it own up? And it could have been any of the five of them, couldn't it?"

"No," Benito said.

"What do you mean, no?" Zoe demanded. "You told me it could."

"That was before we knew about the meat sitting out on that counter. Sandy was standing watch, so he couldn't have been down in the galley at the right time to take it. But as far as the other four go . . ."

Someone knocked on the door and they all looked at it.

"Yes?" Zoe called.

"Zoe, it's Chicken. I'm looking for the captain. He in there?"

Mac opened the door and gestured the cook inside.

Benito moved a little closer to the window. It was getting almost as crowded in here as it got in the crew cabin.

"Sandy tell you about the meat yet?" Chicken asked Mac.

"I guess we kind of beat Sandy to it," Zoe said.

Chicken gave her a reassuring smile. "It's okay, Zoe. I got it figured out. See, it was Jake who tossed it overboard. He was just too lazy to bother wrapping it in plastic so the flies wouldn't be at the garbage. But he'd sure never of thrown it if he'd of known you was down there."

"Jake told you that?" Mac said.

"Well...no. But that's the only thing that adds up, ain't it? See, Jake's a good kid but he *does* get lazy sometimes. He's done stuff like that before. But this time, with him almost getting Zoe killed, I mean, he's too scared to admit he was the one. That's what I figure, at least. And see, Mac, I figure he's so scared that even if you was to talk to him till you was blue in the face, he wouldn't admit it. That's why I decided I'd better tell you."

"I see," Mac said. "Well, thanks for letting me know."

The cook left with a quick nod, his self-satisfied expression saying he felt good about straightening things out.

Mac glanced at Benito. "What do you think?"

He didn't answer, not knowing what to say. Both that mayonnaise and the meat had come from the galley. So the obvious conclusion was that either Chicken or Jake the Rake...but which one? And why?

"Well?" Mac pressed. "You figure Chicken could be right? That it was Jake? And that it was accidental?"

"It's possible," Benito said slowly. It was a damned remote possibility, though. Oh, it could certainly have been Jake. But regardless of Chicken's theory, the ac-cidental part was an *extremely* remote possibility.

"I don't like this, Ben," Mac said. "I don't like to even think about Zoe being—"

"Dad, I'm all right," she interrupted. "And Chicken's theory makes perfect sense, doesn't it?"

Glancing at her, Benito wondered whether she was trying to convince Mac or herself—or both—that she hadn't been an intentional target.

"I don't know what makes sense," the captain muttered. "Zoe, I told you when you arrived I didn't want you aboard the *Yankee* right now. And this sure as hell doesn't make me feel any better about you be-ing here."

Benito was getting the unsettling sense that he knew what Mac was going to say next.

"Look," Mac went on, not quite meeting Benito's gaze, "I realize you've been doing what you prom-ised. If you hadn't been there when that damned shark—"

"What did he promise?" Zoe said, looking at her father suspiciously.

"Well...baby...with this El Gato thing, I wanted to send you straight home. But Ben figured that might tip off the guy. And that might make him run. So we made a deal. I agreed you could stay as long as Ben watched out for you."

"Watched out for me?" Zoe practically shouted. "Like I was two years old? You mean *that's* why he's been breathing down my neck?"

Color suddenly rose to her cheeks. For a second, Benito couldn't figure out why. Then he realized she'd assumed he'd been sticking close because he was in-terested in her.

In your dreams, lady, he said silently, almost laughing. He might have been feeling a twinge of sympathy for her after that shark episode, but the day he was actually interested in Zoe MacLeish would be—

"Baby," Mac said, "I'm sorry, but I want you on the next plane back to California. I don't know what the hell's going on here, but I just can't take the chance."

"Oh, no!" Zoe said. "Oh, no, you don't! You think I'd leave knowing this Cat might come prowling around the *Yankee*? Not knowing what might happen to you if he does? That's absolutely out of the question. I should stay right here. Don't you agree with me, Benito?" she said, turning to him with a look that said, "Help me!"

He gazed into her eyes, her plea for help taking him by surprise. Until this moment, he wouldn't have had trouble believing that she'd never asked anyone for help in her entire life. He just didn't know, though, if convincing Mac to let her stay would be the right thing to do.

If her life was definitely at risk, she'd be better off going. And he didn't know what the hell was happening any more than Mac did.

Worse, that didn't change his basic problem with Zoe's leaving. El Gato would read her sudden departure as meaning exactly what it did mean—that Mac was shipping her off to safety because he was expecting trouble. That might just make El Gato even more determined to proceed. But it *might* send their mastermind high-tailing it and blow this operation.

He didn't want her to go because of that, but he had a gut certainty that if he said she should stay and anything happened to her...well, even though she was a pain, he'd promised her father she'd be safe. If anything happened to her he'd never be able to forgive himself.

"Well?" Mac said. "Who *do* you agree with, Ben?"

Decision time. He'd spent three years chasing El Gato. If he lost him again, how many more crimes would he pull off? How many more people would he kill?

The obvious solution was for Zoe to stay here. But hell, if she did, he was going to have to stick to her even more closely—like it or not.

"Well, Mac," he said, looking evenly at the captain, "I don't think it's a case of agreeing or disagreeing with either of you. I'm just worried that if we overreact we'll jeopardize your agreement with Miguel Lopez. You know how he is. If he gets the idea in his head that you blew our chance at El Gato . . . well, I've heard about him revoking salvage licenses before."

"Lopez might pull your license, Dad?" Zoe said. "If I leave? Well, come on then. The crew would have a collective fit if that happened, so how could you even consider telling me to go?"

Mac scowled.

"If you let her stay," Benito pressed, "I'm sure she won't argue about my watching out for her. In fact," he added, glancing at Zoe, "it wouldn't hurt to act as if you didn't mind my company . . . as if you actually liked me."

Her glare told him what she thought of that idea. He ignored it.

"With her cooperating," he said, turning to Mac again, "I'll be able to make damned sure nothing happens to her. Hell, I'll be able to stick as close as her shadow without anyone being suspicious."

Mac didn't look entirely convinced, but he nodded. "I guess we could give it a try... assuming you'll cooperate, Zoe."

"I can live with it," she muttered.

Benito tried not to grin, but he could see that agreeing almost killed her.

"So, Ben," Mac went on, "where do you figure we should go from here?"

"Well... we'll have to question Marco. Find out what he was looking for in my locker."

"*We?*" Mac said. "I'll do better on my own. Marco might freeze up if you're there."

"Yeah, you're right. You talk to him alone, then. Find out what he was up to and let me know. But look, before you go, what about the rest of the crew? I know you're sure they're all on the straight and narrow, but—"

"Dammit, Ben," Mac said, "we went over this the first day you were aboard ship. Chicken's been with me from the start. Sandy and Marco almost that long. Danny Doyle's been diving for me for over ten years, and Jake's been aboard for five or six. Hell, out of a crew of seven, only two have been with me less than a year."

"Dean Cooper and...?" Benito said, the name of the other permanent diver not coming to him.

"Sam Johnson," Mac supplied. "They both signed on last fall, just before we headed down for that damned salvage operation in South America."

"Did they sign on together? Know each other beforehand?"

"No. They came aboard in different ports. And I trust both of them. Hell, maybe I shouldn't be so damned concerned. After all, there isn't one of my crew I wouldn't trust with my life."

"Yeah...yeah, you've told me that before," Benito said, glancing at Zoe once more, wondering if they could all be trusted with *her* life.

"THE MEAT DIDN'T WORK," Tonto said, leaning on the rail and staring straight ahead.

He knew it would be better to keep quiet, but he couldn't get his mind off what had happened. Since the divers had come up, everybody had been talking about Zoe's near miss.

"I know it didn't work," the Lone Ranger snapped. "I was there, wasn't I?"

Tonto managed not to say anything for a minute, but this wasn't going the way his buddy had told him it would. And the longer it was taking, the more he was thinking they should give up on the plan—before somebody got wise to them. "The mayonnaise didn't work, either," he pointed out.

"It worked perfectly," the Lone Ranger said, glaring along the three feet of rail between them. "She slipped and fell, didn't she? I just didn't luck out on that one."

"And you didn't luck out with the meat, either. So what now?"

"Now it's your turn, little man."

Tonto looked away. He didn't like being called "little man." He wasn't *that* short. And he didn't like the idea of it being his turn, either.

"I don't know," he muttered.

"Don't start giving me a hard time, Tonto. You're in this just as deep as me. And this new idea I've got, well, I'm not in a position to pull it off, but you are."

"I don't know. You're the brains. You're always telling me you're the brains. So if you messed up twice, what makes you figure I'm going to do any better?"

"Dammit, I didn't mess up. Things just didn't quite work out. But they both looked like accidents, didn't they? I told you that's how we'd get away with killing her. And what I've got in mind for you to do is going to look like an accident, too. Just listen to me, Tonto. You do this right and we're a big step closer to the loot."

Chapter Five

Zoe was running through the water. Not swimming, but running. Despite her scuba gear.

"It's all wrong!" a voice inside her head was screaming. "All wrong."

She kept running. Faster and faster, her heart beating so hard it threatened to burst. But each time she glanced back the shark was closer, its teeth longer and sharper.

Terror propelled her even faster.

Suddenly she saw the black hole before her. A cave. Maybe she'd be safe there.

"No!" the voice screamed. "You can't go in there. It might be *the* cave."

She was practically gasping for breath, so she pulled the reserve lever on her regulator. A surge of air rushed through her mouthpiece like a rush of adrenaline into her arteries. It drove her forward the last few feet, to the dark opening.

A moment later she was inside...surrounded by dry air instead of water.

She looked back once more. This time the shark was gone. Everything was gone. All was black. All was silent. Except for the furious thumping of her heart. She was safe . . . or was she?

There was a damp, earthy smell in the cave. A smell she remembered well, one that evoked fresh fear.

It was merely her imagination at work, that had to be all it was. But her heart began beating harder yet. She knew what lived in this cave.

She stood still, waiting . . . knowing they'd find her . . . knowing she couldn't escape.

The sounds became audible then. So soft and low she could scarcely hear them at first, but growing louder.

Cries as faint as whispers in the air. Tiny clicks that echoed everywhere. They were all around her now. Flying all around her in the darkness.

And then she felt one brush against her arm.

She screamed.

"Zoe . . . Zoe . . . Zoe . . ."

Suddenly the darkness was gone. The cries and whispers of the bats were replaced by Billy Bird's reassuring murmurs. Even with half-closed eyes, Zoe could see the orange glow of morning.

Her heart was still racing. Her body was drenched in perspiration. But she'd only been having a nightmare.

"Zoe?" Billy Bird said again. He rubbed her cheek with his head.

"Morning, Billy," she said, opening her eyes. Her fear immediately began to fade in the bright light of day.

Billy strutted along to the end of her berth and sat watching her.

She took a couple of deep breaths, telling herself once more that it had been just a dream. And after yesterday, having a nightmare about a shark attack wasn't surprising.

It had been months, though, since she'd had the one about the Caves of Balancanchén, and she'd been hoping her dreams of them were gone for good.

She'd managed to stop thinking about being in the caves. In fact, she'd managed so well that she could hardly recall the details if she tried. So well, that a psychologist friend had told her she was great at repression.

Zoe doubted he'd meant that as a compliment, but she didn't care. Whatever worked. And refusing to think about the caves certainly had. But repression obviously wasn't as effective when it came to dream time.

She glanced at the clock, then scrambled out of her berth. If she didn't hurry, she'd miss the morning dive.

By the time she'd raced through getting ready and hurried to the equipment room, she'd managed to put the nightmare entirely out of her mind.

"Morning," she said, breezing into the room—a little surprised to find only Danny Doyle and Sam Johnson there. Even though she had to be the last one picking up gear, Marco Vinelli normally issued every piece of diving equipment himself.

"Sorry I'm late," she offered.

Danny merely grinned down at her, telling her he didn't mind.

Sam offered a polite "hello," but it wasn't accompanied by a friendly grin.

As far as she could tell, the sole thing Marco's new diver had in common with Danny was occupation. Well, that and the fact they were both about thirty.

When it came to everything else, they were totally different.

Sam reminded her a lot of Al Pacino. He had a swarthy streets-of-New-York appearance, and was only about her height. Danny was more the clean-cut, Ron Howard type, with red hair that made him seem boyish.

And Danny had always been Mr. Friendly, while she got weird vibes from Sam Johnson. She'd decided he didn't like the idea of a woman being aboard.

"Marco's gone up on deck already," Danny told her. "Left us to wait for you."

She nodded, absently wondering whether Marco was intentionally avoiding her. He had to be hopping mad that she'd told the captain he'd searched Benito's locker. Especially when, as it had turned out, he'd just been trying to help.

He'd overheard her yesterday—telling her father about Benito not being able to identify that coin. She should have realized they hadn't moved far enough down the deck to have a private conversation.

And just as *she* had, Marco had figured the captain was crazy to brush off her suspicions, had figured a little look through Benito's things might turn up something.

"There you go, Zoe," Danny said, handing over her gear.

He and Sam grabbed their larger tanks, then followed her from the equipment room and up into the sunshine on deck.

Marco was standing near the top of the ladder, issuing last-minute instructions as the divers from Cozumel were going down.

"Well, Sam and I gotta get to work, Zoe," Danny said, and the two of them headed over to the rail.

Zoe focused on Marco, finally catching his eye and giving him a wave and one of her best smiles.

Then, while he was still looking at her, she quickly shrugged into her tank harness, resisting the temptation to check her equipment first.

Since Marco personally inspected each piece of diving gear every single time it was going to be used, her checking would only insult him.

Benito, though, obviously wasn't concerned about insulting anyone. He was over by the crane, thoroughly examining his hose connections.

She watched him for a minute, her gaze lingering on his broad shoulders. Whether she liked the man or not, there was no denying he was a hunk.

And actually he wasn't as unlikable as she'd initially thought. Even when they'd been in the middle of that fight yesterday, he'd been reasonable enough to take her side against her father. Otherwise, she'd be on her way home.

And of course, there was nothing like someone's saving you from a shark to improve your opinion of him. She'd certainly been glad he'd known how to use a spear gun.

She swallowed hard and looked away from him. Just the recollection of that water gushing crimson made her shiver—and started her thinking about that darned nightmare again. She began having second thoughts about diving this morning.

Resolutely, she fastened her weight belt, telling herself for the millionth time that Chicken's theory was right. Nobody had been out to get her yesterday. Jake had simply tossed that meat because it was the easiest way to get rid of it. Then he'd been too frightened to confess.

She glanced up at the bridge and spotted her father looking down at her. Lord, she was starting to feel like a goldfish in a glass bowl. Neither he nor Señor Federale, over there by the crane, intended to let her have a moment alone.

"Ready for our buddy-diving?" Benito said, making her jump.

He'd sneaked up without her noticing him, and he was wearing a smug grin.

Seeing it started her annoyance level edging upward. Her opinion of him might have improved, but that didn't mean she liked the way he'd forced her to cooperate with his blasted bodyguard routine.

"I don't need this, you know," she muttered. "Not one bit. I've been diving since I was a child, and the last thing I need is a baby-sitter."

He grinned even more annoyingly and asked if she'd rather be on a plane back to California.

That didn't deserve an answer, so she marched across to the ladder and headed down.

Her bodyguard followed so closely he was practically stepping on her hands. Blast it. He'd been serious about sticking as close to her as her shadow.

They ducked into the silent underwater world and quickly descended to the shoals below.

Enough sunlight penetrated the clear water to make seeing easy at thirty feet, but colors were diffused. Everything was a pale bluish hue—the sandy ocean floor, the fish, the sea growth, even the divers who were beginning their morning's work.

As always, Marco had a supply of extra air tanks lying on one side of the search site, and a school of parrot fish were investigating them.

A couple of the local divers, using hand-held metal detectors, drifted slowly across the sand. The other three started carefully raking through it.

Danny Doyle and Sam Johnson began vacuuming the ocean floor with the air-lift. Its suction hose picked up sand and silt that were then flushed through a strainer to catch small artifacts.

Zoe was certain she'd pinpointed the *Grifon*'s location, which meant there had to be artifacts all over the place, buried under that sand.

About fifty yards to one side of the search site lay a long coral reef. Sometimes, sea growth like that covered sunken objects. The divers had probably checked already, but she wouldn't mind a closer look.

She touched Benito's arm, then gestured at the coral.

They started over, brushing aside the curious fish, and had gone maybe halfway when she began feeling dizzy. She stopped and waited for the sensation to pass.

It didn't. Instead, her body was growing numb and weak and her ears started to ring.

She tried to take a slow, relaxing breath, but her lungs felt constricted. Tiny fingers of panic began tightening around her throat and she pulled for more air.

None came.

Benito had swum on a little, but now he slowly turned in the water and looked back.

Anxiously, she gave him the thumbs-up sign, saying she was going to surface. As he started back toward her, she felt herself growing faint.

She pointed to her mouthpiece and managed to remove it, signaling she needed air. And then her world went black.

ZOE WAS DROWNING. In the blink of an eye she'd started to choke convulsively, had begun sinking in jerky spasms toward the ocean floor. A sea of bubbles poured from her loose mouthpiece and surrounded her.

Benito thrust powerfully with his flippers, but the seconds it took to reach her seemed like hours.

Her long hair was floating up and he grabbed it, pulling her to him. When he saw her face, he realized she'd lost consciousness.

He freed his own mouthpiece and pressed it to her mouth, but she was choking so fiercely he couldn't tell whether she was able to breathe. God, if she'd swallowed too much water, her lungs would be full of it.

Frantically, he gazed back toward the main search area. Most of the divers were busy working, hadn't realized anything was wrong. But one of them was looking over.

For an instant, the man merely stared through the water. Then he swung into action, grabbing one of the extra air tanks and pushing his way through the water with it.

Benito leaned more closely to Zoe again, taking a quick breath from his mouthpiece and returning it to her, wishing he had an extra pair of hands. If she started to struggle it would be game over.

He glanced at the diver again, silently urging him to hurry. Everything underwater seemed to move in slow motion and Zoe could die down here.

Thinking about that started his heart pounding fiercely—so hard it was slamming against the wall of his chest. Each passing moment made him feel more helpless. He was doing the only thing he could think of to do, but if he wasn't doing it right . . .

Then the diver reached them. He shoved the fresh tank at Benito, expertly released Zoe's harness fastenings and slipped her tank off.

In mere seconds, he had the fresh one strapped to her and the regulator's air supply adjusted.

Slinging her used tank over one shoulder, he pointed upward. They weren't deep enough to worry about decompression problems, and with Zoe supported between them, they started quickly to the surface.

Partway there, she regained consciousness and began lashing out at them.

Benito pinned her arms to her sides and held her tightly, waiting for her to realize what was happening and stop struggling.

When she did, they headed the rest of the way up.

They broke the water's surface and Benito shoved off his mask, then tread water while he helped Zoe with hers.

She gasped at the fresh air and started choking again, then began coughing so hard he thought she'd never stop.

Finally, she managed to gain control and slowly shook her head, whispering, "That was a close one."

"You're okay now," he said. "You're going to be okay, Zoe."

The diver asked her in Spanish what had happened. He'd removed his mask, and Benito put a name to the face—Justo Díaz.

"I don't know exactly what went wrong," Zoe murmured, sounding as if she were fighting tears. "I couldn't get air. All of a sudden, I felt as if I were trying to breathe through a straw. I think," she added, glancing at Benito, "I think I might need help getting back to the ship."

"Wrap your arms around my shoulders," he told her. "Don't try to swim. Just hang on."

"I'll come with you," Justo said, this time speaking in English.

By the time the three of them reached the *Yankee*'s ladder, Mac was standing on deck above them, his face as gray as his hair. "What happened?" he yelled down.

Benito shouted that Zoe was okay. "Think you can make it up?" he asked her.

She nodded, then murmured, "Benito?"

"Yes?"

She gave him the most tremulous little smile he'd ever seen and said, "Benito... promise me something?"

"What?"

"Promise that having to save my life isn't going to be a daily occurrence."

For a split second, Benito was seized by an insane urge to hug her. Then he started her up the ladder with a push, feeling an overwhelming sense of déjà vu. He didn't want it to become a habit any more than she did.

He followed right behind her in case she had trouble. When she neared the top, Mac grabbed her arms and pulled her the rest of the way.

Benito hauled himself onto the deck, then turned back to give Justo Díaz a hand, but the diver didn't need help. He was mid-thirties, a couple of years older than Benito and several years older than the other local divers. But he was obviously in good shape.

He still had Zoe's gear slung over one shoulder and slid it across the deck before quickly shrugging out of his own.

Mac had his arms around Zoe, supporting her, but he was looking over her shoulder at Benito, his expression demanding an explanation.

"I don't know," Benito said. "One minute she was fine and the next she was signaling she was in trouble. There must have been something wrong with her air supply."

"*Sí,* that was it exactly," Justo said from behind them.

Benito turned and looked at him. He was kneeling on the deck, examining Zoe's tank.

"What is it, Justo?" Mac said.

"I think you had better look at this, Capitán MacLeish," the diver told him, standing up and holding the tank out to Mac.

"Zoe," Mac said, his voice uneasy, "sit down for a minute, huh, baby?"

"I'm all right," she murmured, drawing free from his arms. "Really, Dad, I'm fine."

Benito moved closer to her. Her face was pale, and she was still breathing raggedly.

He half expected her to collapse and wanted to put his arm around her, but she was so damned independent maybe she'd rather he kept his distance.

He watched her for another minute, though, just in case. Her eyes looked the same luminous green as the water that had almost claimed her. And there was something about the anxiety he saw in them that made him realize she was far more vulnerable than she liked to let on.

"Look at these valves," Justo was saying.

Benito reluctantly pulled his gaze from Zoe to see what the diver was talking about.

Mac was inspecting the tank. After a moment, he swore, then said, "No one except Zoe uses the lighter tanks. This couldn't have been meant for anyone but her."

"What is it?" Benito said.

"The valve that controls cylinder pressure is set all wrong," Justo told him.

"Set," Benito repeated, almost certain he knew what the diver was getting at but hoping he didn't. "You mean it wasn't simply a faulty valve."

"He means someone tampered with it," Mac snapped.

The captain's face was no longer gray. In fact, it was so red he looked as if he were about to explode.

"At thirty feet," Mac went on, a steely edge to his voice, "Zoe would have needed six or seven cubic feet of air a minute to move around easily. This has been set so she couldn't have gotten two."

"And also," Justo said, "someone has jammed the air reserve valve. So she could not just pull the lever and get extra air."

Benito stood staring at the tank, anger gnawing away in his gut. Anger about what had been going on. Anger that Zoe was being made a victim. Anger that he had no idea who was responsible.

"Justo, go back down and send Marco up," Mac ordered. "I've got to get to the bottom of this."

"*Sí,* Capitán," Justo said, grabbing his own tank from the deck.

As he started off, Benito quietly said, "So, Mac? You think it was Marco?"

The captain threw his hands in the air, muttering, "I don't know what to think. All I know is that Marco checks every damned piece of equipment. And he issues it all himself. So I can't see—"

"He wasn't in the equipment room this morning," Zoe said, sorting things out in her mind as she spoke. "Not by the time I got there, I mean. It was Danny who gave me my gear. And Sam Johnson was in there, too."

"Hell," Mac muttered, "we're up to three suspects without even trying, then. And as far as that goes, Marco does his checks early in the morning. Anyone could have gone in and played around with those valves. It wouldn't have taken more than a few seconds."

Zoe was only half listening to her father, thinking more about what she'd just said herself. Sam Johnson had been in the equipment room with Danny.

Maybe, for some reason she couldn't even imagine, it was their Al Pacino look-alike who was trying to kill her. Maybe he didn't like having a woman aboard a whole lot more than she'd realized. Maybe that's why she'd been getting those weird vibes from him.

And that would mean she'd been right all along. None of the old crew would ever do anything to hurt her. That thought made her feel a tiny bit better.

MARCO VINELLI SEEMED too upset to stand still. He kept walking back and forth across the deck, between where Zoe's abandoned scuba tank lay and where she was standing with her father and Benito.

She followed him with her eyes, thinking he couldn't be the one.

Then she noticed the cold way Benito was watching him and wondered if she could possibly be wrong.

"Never, Mac!" Marco said again. "Never in all my years on the *Yankee*. You know how I take care of the equipment. And that something should happen to Zoe..."

He paused and glanced at her as if needing reassurance she was still actually alive. "How could anyone do that?" he went on, gesturing over at her tank. "And who? Danny or Sam! It's just too—"

"What about someone else?" Mac said. "I see almost everyone on board wandering in and out of the equipment room."

"Someone else?" Marco repeated as if the thought hadn't occurred to him. "I...I don't know. Maybe someone else. But I'm going to find out who. And when I do, I'll kill him. With my bare hands."

"Marco," Mac said, "it's not that simple. Whoever did it sure as hell isn't going to admit it. Suppose someone asked you if you'd tried to murder Zoe. What would you say?"

The head diver stopped walking and stood looking at Mac with an expression of disbelief. "Mac, why would someone ask me? You can't possibly think..."

"He doesn't," Zoe said quickly. "None of us do. It's just... it's hard to believe *anyone* would, Marco. And the thought that someone could so easily... it's scary."

"I know," Marco told her. "I can hardly believe it, either. When I left the equipment room this morning your gear was fine. I know it was, because I gave it a quick final check just before I came up."

"Why?" Benito said. "Mac mentioned you do your checks early. Why did you look at Zoe's a final time?"

Marco shot Benito a look that clearly told him to mind his own business, then glanced at Mac.

"It's an obvious question," the captain said.

"And there's an obvious answer, isn't there?" Marco snapped. "I double-checked her gear because of the meat."

"The meat?" Zoe said.

"Zoe, Chicken's story about Jake accidentally throwing that meat overboard is crazy. The crew all know it wasn't any accident. We just don't know who really threw it. And... well, things haven't been too good cuz of that. Not with all of us thinking there's someone on the ship who..."

He paused and gave Benito another look, this one dripping with suspicion.

"He's legit, Marco," Mac said. "How many times do I have to tell you that?"

"Yeah?" Marco said. "Well, it's the first time a government has had someone here waiting to check out a treasure before we've even located it."

"Maybe so," Mac snarled, "but that's the way it is this time. I thought I'd straightened you out on that yesterday. And dammit, Benito's the one who has saved Zoe's life twice. He's not the one who's been trying to kill her."

Marco didn't look entirely convinced. He turned back to Zoe, saying, "The point is, we knew *someone* tried to kill you. And that's why I double-checked your equipment. And I figured if I told both Danny and Sam to wait for you, everything would be okay. Knew they'd kind of be keeping an eye on each other."

"Well look, Marco," Mac said, "tell Danny and Sam I want to talk to them once they come up. But you take it easy on them."

"Yeah, well…" Marco mumbled, backing off along the deck. "Guess I should get back down below and see what's happening. But you just remember, Zoe, you're going to be safe. From now on we'll all be watching out for you."

All except one, she thought, managing a smile for the little diver.

When he turned away, she looked back over at Benito. He and her father were the only two she could be certain were *really* watching out for her.

The thought made her swallow hard. Her father had been watching out for her for twenty-seven years and the habit was ingrained. She wasn't Benito's responsibility, though.

Yet she'd been acting like an absolute witch to him, and he'd been repaying her by saving her life. So the least she could do was try to stop making his life miserable.

"Ben," Mac was saying quietly, "you still worried about not blowing your cover?"

"Of course. I've still got a job to do here, and I don't want word getting out that there's a *federale* on board. It would either scare El Gato off or make him even more careful than usual.''

''Well, if you don't want anyone to know the truth, you'd better take it easy with the questions. In fact, you should probably make yourself scarce around the crew. You're coming on a lot more like a cop than an archaeologist.''

''Yeah,'' Benito muttered. ''I guess you're right. I'm just used to running the show.''

''Well, try to let me handle things. At least make it look as if I am. But can we get back to this mess with Zoe for a minute? Where do we go from here? We've obviously ruled out Marco, so that leaves Danny Doyle and Sam Johnson as our prime suspects, right?''

Zoe was just about to mention those unsettling vibes she got from Sam Johnson when Benito said, ''Don't get carried away, Mac. We don't know for sure that Zoe's gear was fine the last time Marco looked at it.''

''But he said—'' Zoe began.

''Right,'' Benito interrupted. ''He *said*. But odds are about one hundred percent that whoever played with your tank was the same guy who tossed the meat. And neither Danny nor Sam could have done that. They weren't aboard at the time.''

''That's right,'' Mac said. ''They were both on the ocean floor. Working not ten feet from me.''

So much, Zoe thought unhappily, for her Sam Johnson theory.

''But Marco was on board yesterday afternoon,'' Benito went on. ''Supposedly he was checking gear in the equipment room, but he *was* on board. So we sure can't rule him out. In fact, after this incident—''

"Dammit, Ben," Mac interrupted. "How can this be so hard to figure? Why can't we just lay out all the facts and get to the bottom of it? Zoe's had two close calls and we—"

"Three," Benito muttered.

"What?"

Benito cleared his throat, then said, "Mac, let's go talk in your cabin. There's something you don't know about yet."

Chapter Six

Zoe sat on the edge of her father's berth, almost wishing Benito hadn't said anything about her slipping on that mayo yesterday. But then, to figure out who was trying to kill her, they had to consider the entire picture.

It was just that when the captain had learned they hadn't exactly told him the whole truth and nothing but...well, Mac MacLeish angry wasn't a pretty sight.

Even Billy Bird was afraid to open his beak. He was sitting silently on the back of the desk chair with his head tucked under one wing, pretending to be invisible.

"Dammit, Zoe," Mac snapped, making her wince. "I just don't understand why you didn't say something to me right away."

When she looked over to where he was standing by the window, he fixed her with a deadly glare.

"Baby, I don't mean to be hard on you," he continued, his glare a fraction less like a death ray. "Not after what you've been through. But it's normally only you or me who uses the stairs by our cabins, so how in hell could you have thought that mayo got there by accident? And you should have told me what happened immediately.''

"You're right," Benito said.

Anxiously, Zoe glanced across to the other side of the cabin. She was feeling more than a little fragile, and if Benito started in on her too . . .

"Look, Mac," he was saying, "there's no point blaming this on Zoe. She was sure that fall was accidental, but I wasn't. I'm the one who should have told you about it."

"So why the hell didn't you?" Mac said.

"I was wrong, okay? But it's only when we put it together with her other two close calls that it's obvious what happened."

Close calls. That was the second time one of them had used those words. And each time, they'd started something worrying away in Zoe's brain.

"But what was happening wasn't obvious at the time," Benito said. "Besides, the mayo isn't much of a clue when it comes to pointing a finger. It could have been on the floor for hours, which means anyone could have put it there. I figured there was no point getting you worried."

Mac uttered a few choice obscenities, then said, "Somebody's been trying to murder my daughter and I shouldn't get worried?"

Zoe clenched her fists and willed herself not to cry. She never cried. Almost never, at least. But nobody had ever tried to kill her before, let alone three times in two days.

"Dammit, Ben," Mac said, "enough is enough. I don't know who your El Gato is or why he'd want to kill Zoe. But I do know he's got to be the one behind all this. So I want you off my ship. And I want Zoe safely back in California. Now. Before the day is out."

The thought of being back in California no longer struck Zoe as such a bad idea. Her father was right. Enough *was* enough.

"And," he was saying to Benito, "tell Miguel Lopez that if he wants to revoke my license to go right ahead. Let somebody else salvage the *Grifon*. Let somebody else play mouse for your Cat. I've had it."

"I've got news for you, Mac," Benito said evenly. "El Gato has nothing to do with what's been happening to Zoe."

"He *must* have," Zoe said. She gazed over at Benito, certain he was wrong. She'd come to the same obvious conclusion as her father. Somehow, whoever he was, this El Gato character just had to be involved.

"Zoe," Benito said, "there aren't any *musts* here. Not when we don't know what the hell's going on. But I know this much—it's definitely one of the crew who's behind trying to kill you.

"And," he rushed on, holding up his hand as Mac opened his mouth, "it isn't just that El Gato paid one of your guys to do the dirty work, either. He has absolutely nothing to do with this."

"That's crazy!" Mac yelled. "Completely crazy! I'll bet El Gato has a whole damned lot to do with it. Because none of my crew would have thought up trying to kill Zoe. Dammit, we're not talking *Mutiny on the Bounty* or something, here. I've been captain of a salvage ship for more than thirty years. And nothing like this ever happened until I got roped into this insane plan to catch your crook."

"Mac," Benito said, "I started out thinking the same way you are. But the more I thought, the clearer it was that El Gato can't be responsible. What possible reason could he have for wanting Zoe to die?"

"I don't know! I just told you, I don't know why he'd want to kill her, but—"

"Well, Mac, listen to me, because I'm going to tell you why he *wouldn't*. Just think like El Gato for a minute. He's after the *Grifon*'s treasure, so he wants you to locate the wreck. He wants you to raise that treasure, get it all together for him in your strong room. Then he can just walk in and take it. You with me so far?"

"Dammit, Ben, I know all that. Get to the point."

"The point is that if somebody killed your daughter, you'd be mighty upset, wouldn't you? So upset you'd likely say what you just said—'Let somebody else salvage the *Grifon*.' Right?"

"Of course it's right, but—"

"And where would that leave El Gato, Mac? Cooling his heels, that's where. Having to put his plan on ice until Lopez awarded the salvage license to someone else. Until some new captain got his act together. So would it be smart of El Gato to do anything to interrupt your search? Would it?"

"No," Mac snapped.

"Right, it would be dumb. And I guarantee you, El Gato is one smart customer."

Mac pounded his hand with his fist and unleashed a few more obscenities, while Zoe uneasily considered Benito's logic. It made sense ... and if El Gato wasn't the one who'd come up with the idea of killing her, then one of the crew must have ... unless ...

"Mac," Benito said quietly, "El Gato has absolutely no reason for wanting Zoe dead, but somebody obviously does. Somebody aboard this ship."

"What if . . . ?" Zoe said tentatively.

"What if what?" Benito asked.

"What if somebody figured out a way to get on and off the *Yankee* without being noticed?"

"Baby, you know we stand twenty-four-hour watch," Mac said.

"I know." Zoe glanced from her father to Benito. "But what if you're wrong about El Gato not being involved? What if he *has* paid someone off, and whoever it is has been letting him come and go?"

"No," Mac said firmly. "Somebody would have noticed a stranger for sure. But what about the divers from Cozumel?" he asked, turning to Benito. "I know you were thinking that maybe one of them . . ."

"Uh-uh. I mean, it's possible El Gato might use one of them for something. But they can't have had anything to do with Zoe's *accidents*. Every time something's happened to her, they've been diving. Mac, I know you don't like the idea but look, you've only got seven guys. So let's figure out which of them—"

A knock on the door interrupted them.

"Yeah?" Mac called.

"It's Danny, Mac. And Sam. Marco said you wanted to talk to us."

"Yeah. Come in here."

Zoe's discomfort level edged up a notch. As far as she knew, Miss Manners had never given advice on how to act around people who might have tried to murder you.

But when she saw Danny and Sam, she realized her discomfort level had nothing on theirs. They both looked as if they were terrified the captain intended to keelhaul them.

Then she glanced at her father and realized that if either of them said the wrong thing, he probably would.

"Leave us," Mac ordered, looking pointedly at Benito, clearly reminding him he was supposed to play archaeologist, not cop.

Without a word, Benito started for the door, Zoe on his heels.

Without a peep, Billy darted through the air and out of the cabin ahead of them.

ZOE HAD BEEN TEMPTED to stay right outside her father's cabin, with her ear to the door, to listen to every word Danny Doyle and Sam Johnson said. But Benito had headed for the deck so she'd followed him, hoping he'd figured things out a little more than she had.

As much as she hated puzzles, solving this one was a matter of life and death. *Her* life and death. That thought didn't just make her blood run cold, it practically froze her veins solid.

Benito finally stopped walking and sank sideways onto a lounge chair.

Zoe sat down facing him on the one next to it and waited for a good half minute. Until she couldn't stand the silence any longer.

"Well?" she demanded. "You think Dad's going to get anywhere with Danny and Sam?"

"What I think, Zoe, what I keep coming back to, is that neither of them could have thrown that meat overboard. So I think we should still be concentrating on the five guys who were aboard then."

"On all five? But we already decided it couldn't have been Sandy. We know he was standing watch when the meat disappeared from the galley."

"That's true," Benito said slowly. "It couldn't have been Sandy."

Benito's agreeing made her feel a little better. And if they could eliminate some of the others, she'd feel a *whole lot* better. "And Dean Cooper was in the strong room, working on his camera," she tried.

"Well, that's like Marco claiming he was in the equipment room. Could be it's true, but could be it isn't. And both Jake and Chicken say they were off on their own. No witnesses."

"You mean Sandy is the only one we can really rule out? We're left with four suspects?" Zoe watched Benito, waiting for his reply, praying they weren't actually left with four—that he'd rule out three more in short order.

She didn't want four suspects. She wanted one guilty party. And she wanted him arrested and off the *Yankee*. Then her father wouldn't hustle her back to California and this would turn into a normal summer.

But Benito didn't say a word about ruling out anyone. Instead, he reached across and took her hand.

That surprised her so much she just sat staring at him.

He glanced down at their hands for a second, then looked up and shrugged, saying, "I . . . you seemed so damned upset, Zoe. Sorry," he added, releasing his hold. "I didn't mean anything personal by that, just . . . well, sorry."

"Ahh . . ." She told her brain to slow down. It was whirling far faster than thinking-and-talking speed.

Maybe she hadn't liked Benito at first, but somewhere along the line she'd changed her mind. It probably had a lot to do with the way he'd whisked her from the jaws of death. But whatever the reason, she'd started to like him. And she'd certainly liked the strong, reassuring feel of his hand holding hers.

She was still trying to think of what to say when Billy Bird flew along and landed, with a noisy flap of his wings, on the end of her lounger.

Benito eyed the bird intently.

"Billy's got something again," he said, reaching across. "A ring, this time."

"Mine!" Billy shrieked, dropping the ring but raising one foot, talons splayed to strike.

Benito jerked back his hand, saying, "Damned bird."

"Billy," Zoe said sternly, "you give me that."

"Mine!"

"No wonder parrots are an endangered species," Benito muttered.

"Billy, you give me that," Zoe repeated, injecting a threat into her tone. Now that she'd had a glimpse of the ring, she was darned curious about it.

The bird shot her the kind of evil look he usually reserved for others, but he edged a couple of inches away from his treasure.

Zoe grabbed it before he had second thoughts and sat gazing at it, a dozen different questions racing through her mind. She didn't think she'd seen the ring before, yet there was something familiar about it.

The piece was priceless. Ancient . . . a man's heavy gold ring, laced with intricate jade work and etched with a design she should recognize . . . thought she *did* recognize...she couldn't think where she'd seen it before, though.

It was from the Yucatán, that much she knew. But it was from a specific place, and for some reason her mind was blocking on exactly where.

"Billy," she said, glancing back at him, "where did you get this?"

"Captain Mac," he said sullenly.

"Stupid bird," Benito said. "He didn't take it from Mac's cabin. He wasn't holding anything when we left."

"No," Zoe explained, "he doesn't necessarily mean he just got it from there now. Sometimes he takes things and hides them to play with later. But this isn't one of the souvenirs Dad leaves sitting out."

"Maybe you just haven't seen it before," Benito suggested. "Maybe it's something he got over the winter."

"No...no, he was in South America all winter, and this is from right around here. It's Mayan. From the Yucatán peninsula. I just...I should be able to tell you exactly where, but it isn't coming to me."

"Doesn't matter."

"I'm not so sure about that," Zoe said slowly. "This ring is museum quality. *Extremely* valuable. I can't believe Dad wouldn't have shown it to me the minute I arrived. And I'm certain he wouldn't just leave it sitting around. Especially not when Billy is forever getting into his things."

"Maybe it isn't your father's," Benito said, looking at it with obvious interest now. "Maybe Billy was lying about where he got it."

Billy Bird puffed up his feathers and screeched, "Billy doesn't lie!"

"We know you don't, Billy," Zoe said. "He doesn't," she added quietly, glancing at Benito again. "Birds really aren't very smart. They don't understand the concept of lying. If he says he got it from Dad's cabin, that's where he got it."

Benito rubbed his jaw thoughtfully, wondering whether this latest little mystery could have anything to do with the big picture. "You're sure the ring's really valuable?" he asked.

"Incredibly."

"Well, then, if it came from your father's cabin, I guess maybe we should be asking how it got there. Let's go try that on him."

Zoe nodded and held out her arm to Billy Bird. He hopped onto it as if it were a perch.

On the way to Mac's cabin, thoughts he didn't like began nagging at Benito. What if the captain wasn't quite the man he seemed to be?

There were a lot of Mayan ruins in Mexico that the government didn't have funds to excavate. Some of them contained rare jewels and other artifacts that would ultimately end up in museums. Unless treasure hunters got to them first.

The country had a serious problem with its ancient pyramids and temples being plundered, and national treasures being stolen and smuggled out of Mexico. El Gato had pulled off a few of those sorts of heists himself.

So if that ring of Billy Bird's was museum quality, how had Mac gotten hold of it?

Benito glanced at Zoe, his nagging thoughts multiplying.

He could hardly turn a blind eye if Mac MacLeish was into something criminal. He'd have to follow up.

But what the hell was he going to do if he found out the salvage captain had an illegal sideline?

Arrest him on the spot? Wait until they'd nailed El Gato, then reward Mac for his help by tossing him into jail? And how would Zoe take it, either way?

Damned stupid question, he said silently as they reached Mac's cabin.

The door was standing open. Danny and Sam were gone—probably down having lunch with the rest of the crew—but Zoe was apparently more interested in finding out about the ring than in hearing what they'd told her father.

"Look what Billy was playing with this time," she said the moment they walked in.

Billy Bird flapped from her arm over to Mac's desk and sat watching, his beady little eyes following the ring as Zoe handed it over.

Mac gazed at it, shaking his head, saying, "I wonder where he got this? I've never seen it before."

"Then Billy didn't know what he was talking about after all," Benito said, hoping Mac wasn't merely acting.

He had a gut feeling the captain was an honest man. But with that damned bird saying…he looked over at Billy with annoyance, then immediately felt like a fool.

Of course the thing didn't know what it was talking about. It was just a stupid bird. When had he started believing it had more than a bird brain?

"This doesn't add up," Zoe was saying slowly. "Why would Billy tell us he got it from you, Dad, if—"

"I don't know why," Mac said. "But he didn't. So where *did* you get it?" he demanded, looking over at the bird.

"Captain Mac," Billy said, strutting across the desk. "Captain Mac."

"That's enough nonsense," Mac snapped. "You didn't get it from me."

The captain looked so damned mad that Benito almost laughed. So Zoe had been wrong. Birds *did* understand the concept of lying. Because if they didn't...

That nagging worry came creeping back into his mind. What if Zoe *hadn't* been wrong? If birds really weren't very smart, if they *didn't* understand about lying, then Billy had found that ring in this cabin. Regardless of what Mac was saying.

Benito shelved his unsettling thoughts about Mac for future consideration. There were getting to be so many mysteries around here it looked like he was going to have to prioritize them. And at the moment, what had been happening to Zoe beat out worrying about how Mac had come by the damned ring.

"Let's leave trying to find out where the ring came from for later," he said. "Mac, where did you end up with Danny Doyle and Sam Johnson?"

"Nowhere. I mean, they both said nobody came into the equipment room after Marco left. Not until Zoe arrived. So either Marco was lying about that tank being fine when he last checked it, or Danny and Sam were lying about nobody else coming in."

"Or one of *them* fiddled with the tank and the other didn't notice," Benito muttered. "You said it would only take a few seconds."

Mac ran his fingers through his hair, looking as frustrated as Benito felt.

"We're never going to figure out what's going on, are we?" Zoe said.

Benito glanced at her and immediately regretted it. Her eyes were wide and frightened, and she was watching him as if she were hoping he had a magic trick up his sleeve. It made him wish to hell he did.

She held his gaze for a moment, then wandered over to her father's berth and sat down, murmuring, "Couldn't we be missing a clue here? Something we haven't thought of?"

Benito racked his brain, reaching into every one of its dusty recesses, trying to come up with an angle that might give them the something else she wanted.

Everything he thought of struck him as ludicrous, but sometimes it was what seemed most bizarre that ended up providing a key.

"Look," he finally said, "unless we've got a homicidal maniac aboard, whoever our guy is has a motive for what he's been doing. So let's try something completely off the wall. Zoe, is there anyone, anywhere, who'd be happy to see you dead? I mean, even in California?"

"What the hell's California got to do with this?" Mac said. "She's here, not there."

"Dammit, Mac, I don't know what anything has to do with anything. I'm reaching for straws. And this is probably the thinnest straw going, but there's always the possibility of a contract killing."

"What?" Zoe whispered.

"I said *possibility*," Benito told her quietly, almost wishing he'd kept that particular straw to himself. "El Gato wouldn't have paid off one of the crew to kill you. But it's possible someone else did."

"That sounds like a damned farfetched possibility," Mac muttered.

Benito shrugged, then glanced at Zoe again.

She was looking even more upset than she'd been before. All he'd done by raising that ridiculous idea was make things worse. He felt like kicking himself.

"Benito?" she murmured.

"What?"

"I was just...no, it's so silly it isn't worth mentioning."

"Mention it."

"Well...a contract killing. It really *is* silly. I mean the thought of anybody putting a contract out on someone like me. But something happened just before I left California. It can't possibly be connected, though. I never really thought he might have been trying to—"

"Let's hear what happened," Benito said, his adrenaline starting to pump, his instinct telling him this wasn't going to be as silly as Zoe figured.

"Well...it was the evening before I got here," she said. "I'd seen that article about the *Grifon* in the paper and realized Dad was up to something. So I called around looking for a flight to Cozumel and booked one out of L.A. first thing in the morning. But the traffic there is so deadly in rush hour that I decided to drive down right away, stay near the airport overnight."

"And?" Mac prompted.

"And I was almost ready to leave when someone knocked on my door. But nobody'd buzzed from the lobby, so I checked through the peephole. And it was a man I didn't know, and I was in a hurry to get going, so I didn't even ask what he wanted, just pretended I wasn't in. A few minutes later, I went down to the garage."

"And?" Mac said again.

"And...and he was down there, walking slowly between one of the rows of cars, looking at each of them. Then he realized I was watching him and just stared at me for a second...as if he recognized me. And then he started across the garage toward me. But my parking space is right by the elevator, so I jumped into the car and took off."

Benito nodded, trying to keep his face expressionless. But hadn't Zoe realized the guy was looking for *her* car? Looking to see if she really might be at home? Or maybe intending to tamper with her car if it was there?

She was gazing at him anxiously, so he said, "Go on, Zoe. What happened after you took off?"

"Nothing. I mean, I don't think he followed me or anything. I kept checking the rearview."

"And you're sure he wasn't someone you knew? Not even slightly?"

"Benito, I didn't remember ever seeing his face before. I decided he was just some weirdo and put the whole thing out of my mind. I haven't thought of it at all, since. I'm kind of good at repressing things. But earlier, when you and Dad were talking about my close calls, it started me wondering."

"Good God," Benito muttered, his stomach clenching. Looking at Zoe made it almost impossible to think about somebody trying to kill her. But somebody—or somebodies all over the damned place, from the sound of this—*had* been.

"Ben?" Mac said. "You don't really think...not a contract killing...do you?"

"I'm not sure. But it sounds like a typical scenario. Somebody wants you dead. And one day you open your door and you're looking into the barrel of a stranger's automatic. Or you're getting in or out of your car in an isolated parking garage and suddenly it's game over.''

"But who?'' Zoe whispered, gazing at Benito as if he might actually know the answer.

She looked so frightened that he crossed the cabin and sat down on Mac's berth beside her, saying, "Can you think of anyone at all who'd benefit if you were out of the picture? What about your will? You don't have a million dollars you've willed to someone, do you?''

"Oh, Benito,'' she murmured, her voice full of tears. "I don't have a red cent. All I have is some furniture and a five-year-old car. And as far as my will goes, Dad's my beneficiary.''

"Then what about a different motive?'' Benito suggested. "Something other than money. Anyone hate you, Zoe? Want revenge for something?''

"I don't know,'' she murmured. "I mean, no, not anyone I know about.''

Mac paced across the cabin and stood in front of them, staring down at Benito. "Ben, exactly where the hell are we here? This contract business...none of this makes sense to me.''

Benito looked at Zoe again, about to say that none of it made sense to him, either, but she looked so damned scared he had to sound as if he had some answers.

"Well,'' he said slowly, "where we are is that somebody wants Zoe dead. And whoever it is could have sent that guy to her apartment. Then, when she unexpectedly took off and came here, that somebody could have contracted one of the crew to make the hit.''

"That doesn't seem possible," Mac said. "How could it happen so fast? Zoe barely got here before things started happening."

Benito nodded. There *was* a timing flaw to the theory, and Mac had zeroed in on it.

"You're right, Mac," he finally said. "First the guy would have had to find out where Zoe had gone. Then he'd have had to find out about the crew—figure out who might go for the plan. And from what you've said, if he'd approached most of your men they'd have told you about it."

"They'd have killed the guy on the spot," Mac snapped.

"Dammit," Benito muttered to himself, "there's something I just can't put my finger on. How could things possibly... it's almost as if..."

"Go on," Mac said.

Benito gazed at Zoe, needing another few seconds to let the logic fall into place, then he glanced back at Mac, saying, "Let's turn this around. I was thinking the contract originated in California and followed Zoe here. But what if it originated here?"

"I... I don't understand," Zoe said.

"I mean, what if it was someone on the *Yankee* who wanted you killed in the first place? Your father told the crew you'd be staying in California longer than usual this spring, so our guy arranged for the hit to go down there. But suddenly you arrived here and—"

"Good God, Ben!" Mac roared so loudly that Billy Bird gave a squawk and flapped down from the desktop to the floor.

"You're back to the crew again," Mac went on more quietly. "And if you get back to them, then what about the motive? None of my crew would gain a thing from killing Zoe. Not unless they killed me, too, of course. And that idea's too preposterous even to think about."

"What?" Benito said, not quite able to believe what he'd heard.

"What?" he repeated when Mac didn't answer.

But the captain wasn't paying any attention to the question. He was staring at Billy Bird. "What the hell's the damned bird up to?" he said.

Billy was standing on the floor beside Mac's desk, bobbing his head back and forth at it.

The desk's solid sides and back extended almost to the floor, clearing it by only a few inches, and Billy finally poked his head into that narrow space.

When he drew it back out, he was holding something gold in his beak.

"Good God," Mac said, bending down to take it. "It's another ring. Look at this one, Zoe," he added, tossing it over to her.

She examined it for a moment, then said, "It's almost identical to the other one. Right down to the design in the etching. Lord, I wish I could think where they originally came from, but I'm still drawing a blank."

While she was speaking, Mac had dropped to his hands and knees and started feeling around under the desk.

"I don't believe this," he muttered. "Somebody's screwed three hooks in under here. And will you look at this!"

He shoved himself up off the floor with one hand and held the other one out to them. Lying on his palm was a third matching ring.

Benito stared at it, then looked at Mac's face. The man seemed truly flabbergasted. Either those rings being there were a surprise to him or he was one hell of an actor.

So what was the truth here? Was Mac a crook or not?

A few moments thought, a little logic, a lot of gut instinct, and Benito decided the answer was *not*. He'd gone off track with that suspicion.

If Mac actually had anything to do with those rings, he'd have been damned careful to hide them someplace where Billy could never get at them. That had to mean somebody else had hidden them there. But who? And why?

Hell, coming up with those answers was bound to take some hard figuring. And they'd left another question hanging that was a damned sight more important.

He caught Mac's eye and told him to forget about the rings for a minute. "Get back to what you said before," he added.

"What?"

"Something about none of the crew gaining from killing Zoe unless they killed you, too."

"Oh, yeah, but like I said, that idea's too preposterous to even think about."

Benito just kept staring at Mac until the penny dropped.

The captain's face suddenly paled.

Zoe had clicked in, as well. She was gazing wide-eyed at her father.

"Mac," Benito muttered, "I think you'd better start elaborating on that one."

Chapter Seven

"You screwed up, Tonto."

"I didn't," he snapped angrily. The Lone Ranger had made two tries and blown them both, so who the hell was he to talk? "It was that Mexican government dude. If he wasn't there she'd have drowned."

"But he was there. And she didn't drown. Damn, it was so simple and you screwed up. No wonder I call you Tonto."

"What? What's that supposed to mean?"

The Lone Ranger smiled an unfriendly smile, saying, "You don't even know that much do you? Just *shows* how stupid you are. You don't know what Tonto means in Spanish?"

Tonto shook his head.

"It means *stupid,* you stupid little man."

Tonto clenched his fists but didn't raise them. He knew the Lone Ranger was too good in a fight ... no, he wouldn't call him the Lone Ranger anymore. They wouldn't be buddies anymore. Maybe they wouldn't even be partners. Maybe he wouldn't even show him what he had ... or maybe he would. That would prove he wasn't stupid.

He glanced along the deck. The others were getting their gear on for the afternoon dive, so if he was going to do any showing it had to be now. "Look at this," he said, pulling the two gold coins from the pocket of his trunks. "I found them during this morning's dive."

His partner snatched them from him and stared at them. "From the *Grifon*?"

"I think so."

"Did you let anyone else see them?"

"Of course not. I'm not *stupid*. Even though some people maybe think so."

"This means we're damn close then," his partner said, ignoring the clever remark. "We'll find the main wreck any dive now."

"How *smart* of you to figure that out," Tonto said. He grinned at his own wit, feeling better.

"This means we have to get Zoe fast, then."

"How?"

"I don't know. But I'll do something, Tonto. I'll get her somehow."

BILLY BIRD WAS PERCHED on the edge of Mac's desk, his head tucked under one wing, playing his invisible game.

Watching him made Zoe want to crawl between the sheets on her father's berth and hide. But she knew that pretending to be invisible just wouldn't chase reality away as it seemed to do for Billy.

And reality, assuming Benito's line of reasoning was right, said that not only was one of the crew trying to kill *her*, but that he intended to murder her father, as well.

The thought of anything happening to him had gotten her even more upset than she'd already been. Every time she looked at him now, tears threatened to spill over. So she simply sat staring at the floor of his cabin while he finished telling Benito the details of his will.

It was the first she'd ever heard about its terms, but they didn't surprise her. Looking out for his crew's interests was typical of Mac MacLeish.

But it seemed that one of the crew wasn't concerned about looking out for the captain's interests.

Or yours, either, Zoe, a tiny voice in her head reminded her, sending an icy shiver up her spine.

She glanced over at Benito. Earlier, he'd been sitting on the berth with her, but now he was pacing back and forth across the confined space of the cabin.

His gaze caught hers for a moment, his dark eyes filled with concern, and she was struck by the most desperate desire to have him sitting right beside her again. Irrational as it might be, that had made her feel better.

He apparently wasn't tuned into her wavelength, though, because he kept right on pacing and turned his attention back to her father.

"All right, Mac," he said, "I want to be entirely clear on this. Zoe is your sole beneficiary. But if she predeceases you..."

She closed her eyes, but that didn't work any better than pulling a sheet over her head would have. The words *predeceases you* started flashing on and off in her mind like a neon sign. They were right up there on the list of phrases she'd begun to hate. Right up there with *be murdered* and *get killed.*

Predeceases you was the worst, though. It implied they'd both die—she before her father. She blinked back tears and concentrated on Benito's words.

"If Zoe predeceases you," he was saying again, "your estate will be shared by the crew."

Mac nodded, his expression morose. "Aside from Zoe...well, those guys are a damned sight closer to me than the few distant relatives I've got."

"But *one* of those guys..." Benito muttered.

He didn't finish the thought. He didn't have to.

"And how large each man's share would be," he went on, "depends on his length of service aboard the *Yankee*."

"Yeah," Mac said. "The lawyer worked out some formula for that. So the way things stand now, Chicken would get the most because he's been with me the longest. Then Marco and Sandy. Then Danny...Jake the Rake. And Dean Cooper and Sam Johnson would get something, but not nearly as much as any of the others."

"And they all know about the terms."

"Well...yeah, I guess they do. I mean, way back when the will was written I told the crew what it said. But that was a long time ago, just a few years after my wife died. Some of the guys who were with me then are gone now, and I don't recall mentioning anything about it to the newer ones. It's not something I ever think about. Never has been until now, at least."

"So," Benito said, "way back when, you'd have told Chicken, Sandy and Marco, right?"

"Right."

"What about Danny Doyle?"

"No. Danny signed on later. Jake, too. But…well, I guess one of the others might have mentioned it to them. And to Dean and Sam."

"I'd say that's a pretty good guess," Benito said. "And now you're on the verge of locating a fifty-million-dollar treasure. And the government takes half, but you get to keep half. A cool twenty-five mill."

Mac shook his head, saying, "I don't get to keep it all myself. Salvaging is an expensive business. I have investors who get part of it. And each of the crew gets a portion. See, they work for virtually no wages, and whenever there's a payoff we all share in it. We've just never had one anywhere near this size to share before."

"You, Mac, though," Benito pressed. "You, personally. About how much of that twenty-five million would be yours?"

"I don't know exactly. Maybe about half."

Benito whistled a long, low whistle.

"Dammit, Ben," Mac muttered. "It never occurred to me one of them might not be loyal. Never even occurred to me. How could I have been so stupid?"

"You weren't being stupid, Mac. It's just that so much money does strange things to some men's loyalties."

"But which one?" Mac said. "Which one?"

Zoe cleared her throat, not sure her voice was in working order, and the two men looked at her.

"You're both certain it's one of the crew, aren't you?" she said. "I mean, this theory about one of them killing us so he'll get a share of Dad's estate... you're absolutely certain that explains what's been going on?''

''It makes sense out of the entire mess,'' Benito told her.

She nodded slowly. After all the time they'd spent trying to make sense of things, she should probably feel glad they'd finally succeeded.

Instead, what she felt was ill and frightened. Ill at the thought that someone they knew and trusted wanted them dead. And frightened at the thought that the someone might get what he wanted.

''Perfect sense,'' Benito was saying quietly, as if to himself. ''One of them arranges a contract on you in California. Suddenly, though, you're not in California, you're here. And he's left to his own devices.''

Zoe sat wishing Benito had spoken even more quietly—so that she hadn't heard him. Reading murder mysteries was one thing, but listening to someone talk about your own murder... only if they knew who the *someone* was, no one would be murdered. Not her, not her father.

''Benito, you're the expert here,'' she said, her voice quavering just a little. ''Who do you think...?''

''My money,'' he said slowly, ''has to be on Chicken or Jake. Except when they're off getting supplies, they're always on board. Both the mayo and the meat came from the galley. And the idea of Marco being the one who tampered with your tank, Zoe, just strikes me as being too damned obvious.''

Mac raked his fingers through his hair. ''So what do I do, Ben? I can't toss both Chicken and Jake off the *Yankee* when one of them's innocent. And we aren't even positive it's one of them who's guilty. We've got to figure out for sure who is. But in the meantime,'' he added, looking over at Zoe, "I want you off the ship. I want you someplace you'll be safe."

She didn't say anything. What was there to say when he was right? The *Yankee* with a killer aboard was anything but safe . . . for her *or* her father.

Knowing him, though, she was going to have one hell of a time convincing him to abandon ship.

"What place did you have in mind, Mac?" Benito said.

Mac glanced at him with a puzzled expression.

"The someplace Zoe will be safe, I mean. After what happened right in her own apartment building, we have to rule out her going home. And anywhere else she went . . . well, she'd be pretty much on her own, wouldn't she? So someplace safe has to mean someplace where nobody could find her."

Benito's gaze drifted over to Zoe as he finished speaking. She looked terrified and he didn't blame her. She was definitely in danger here. But what if she left and their killer tracked her down? She wouldn't have a chance.

At least while he was protecting her . . . or was he kidding himself?

That shark had almost finished her. And only a few hours ago, she'd practically drowned. What if the next time something happened he wasn't right there? Or wasn't fast enough or smart enough or strong enough? Yet the thought of her being alone and afraid . . .

Maybe, dangerous as it might be, the best place for her was right here. He'd just have to make sure there *was* no next time.

"Someplace where nobody could find her." Mac repeated the phrase slowly. "Did you have a place in mind, Ben?"

He wanted to choose his words carefully, didn't want to say anything that would frighten Zoe even more, but his brain seemed determined to think in Spanish and the right words in English just wouldn't come.

Or maybe there were no right words. Not in either language.

Finally, he gave up trying and said, "Mac...I don't think there's a place in the world where a person can't be found. Not if someone wants to find them badly enough."

"Good God, man," Mac snapped. "You aren't suggesting she stay aboard."

"Dad..." Zoe said.

The one tiny word positively quivered, and Benito wished he'd never opened his damned mouth.

"Dad," she began again, "if I go, you'll leave, too, won't you? Leave Sandy in command and come with me, I mean?"

"Oh, baby, I know you'd be frightened on your own, but it wouldn't be for long. Just until Ben and I figure out who's been behind this and turn him over to—"

"No," she said, shaking her head firmly. "Dad, I don't want to leave you here. There's not only what's happened to me. There's El Gato, as well. If I left without you, all I'd do would be worry about you."

"Baby, don't be crazy. I can take care of myself. But you—"

"I can take care of myself, too! What do you think I do from September to May every year? And I know how to use a gun."

Benito exhaled slowly, remembering Zoe pulling that gun on him, remembering how easy it had been to disarm her.

Dammit to hell, this was a no-win situation. She wasn't safe aboard the *Yankee*, but if their killer was persistent she wouldn't be safe off it, either.

But what his real problem came down to, the thing that had sent him reeling when it finally sank into his thick skull, was that he wanted her here so he could do everything in his power to... What he couldn't figure out, though, was exactly when he'd started worrying about her as if she were somebody he loved, not just somebody it was part of his job to protect.

He'd never gotten personally involved in a case until now, and it went against all his training. But despite her hot temper, despite her damned stubbornness, despite the fact that she could be the worst pain-in-the-butt he'd ever met, something about Zoe MacLeish had gotten to him in a way he wouldn't have believed possible. And he sure as hell wasn't going to let her die.

"Dad," she was saying, "I know my staying would be risky. But if I leave, where am I going to go? Benito just said there's no place a person can't be found."

"But, Zoe, if you were here you—"

"No, listen. Remember what Marco said? The whole crew is watching out for me so I'll be safe."

"Zoe," Mac snapped. "Come off it."

"Well, *almost* the whole crew, Dad. I could keep your Colt with me at night, and your cabin is right across the passageway."

"Oh sure, baby. All you're forgetting is that I sleep sounder than a dead man."

"Well...Billy Bird can shriek louder than any alarm system. He'd wake you up."

Mac sat running his fingers through his hair again, clearly considering. And Benito knew exactly what the captain was trying to decide. Was Zoe's facing a definite danger, with three of them to watch out for it, better or worse than her facing the possibility of danger on her own?

"Well, Ben?" Mac finally said. "What do you think? If you were me, what would you do?"

"I'd send her packing in a second, Mac—*if* I felt certain she'd be safe."

"But you don't."

Benito shook his head.

The captain pushed himself from the chair and stood staring out the window for a minute, then turned back and gazed evenly at Benito. "I'm going to ask you something, Ben, and I want a totally honest answer."

"All right."

"Ever since Zoe arrived and I said I didn't want her aboard, you've been telling me that if she left it would probably tip off your Cat that we were expecting him."

"I still figure it would. What I don't know is whether that would make him back off or just come on stronger. You never know which way he'll jump."

"Well...my question is, how much does worrying about losing your shot at El Gato have to do with your thinking that maybe Zoe should stay aboard now?"

Benito glanced at Zoe and realized it no longer had the slightest damned thing to do with his thinking. If he could be certain she'd be safe off the *Yankee*, he'd gladly spend another three years tracking El Gato.

"HE'S GOING TO MAKE me leave," Zoe said. "The only reason he told me he'd think it over was so he'd have time to figure out where to send me."

Benito looked along the foot of railing between them. Zoe was gazing out across the water toward Cozumel.

He watched her for a moment. The way the breeze was playing with her long dark hair made him want to reach over and smooth it with his hand.

The only time he'd ever touched her hair was underwater. Dry, it likely felt like silk. But the way things were shaping up, he'd never know. Zoe was going to be out of his life as suddenly as she'd entered it.

"Just wait and see," she murmured, still staring at the island's coastline. "The afternoon dive won't even be over before he'll bundle me into the launch. Maybe I should go down and cut it loose."

"I don't think that would get you anywhere. Mac would just send you off on the boat that comes to pick up the local divers."

"Well, then, maybe I should go down and take off, before he can order me someplace."

"I think you'd need the ignition key," Benito pointed out.

Zoe gave him a look that told him she wasn't in the mood to be teased and said, "Dad always leaves a spare key in the glove compartment."

Benito glanced toward the *Yankee*'s stern, to where the motorboat was tied, and almost smiled at the thought of Mac's face if he found his launch had vanished. But there really wasn't much to be smiling about.

"Zoe," he said, turning back to her, "wherever Mac decides he wants you to go . . . well, maybe your leaving would be for the best. You aren't safe here. You know that.''

She looked at him then, catching his gaze in the deep green of her eyes. "But I'm not safe anywhere, am I? That's what you said. And if that's the case, I'd far rather be here with Dad . . . and you.''

Her eyes held his another fraction of a second, then she gazed out over the Caribbean once more.

He tried to ignore the crazy idea that seemed intent on taking over his mind, but it just kept getting stronger. The crazy idea that if she left he could go with her and make damned sure she was safe wherever Mac sent her.

He had weeks of vacation time backed up, so if he could convince his superiors to let someone else wait here for El Gato . . . and she'd only need watching out for until Mac learned who was behind the murder plot.

"Oh my Lord," she whispered, turning to him as she spoke.

"What?"

"Benito, those rings in Dad's cabin. I just realized why they seemed so familiar. I think I *have* seen them before.''

"Where?"

She shook her head, looking incredibly upset.

"Zoe?" He put his hands on her bare arms and gazed at her. "Zoe, what's the matter?"

"I . . . nothing. It's just something stupid that happened last summer. I have nightmares about it sometimes so I try not to think of it. That must be why I didn't remember right away.''

"Didn't remember *what?*"

"Have you heard of the Caves of Balancanchén?''

He simply stared at her, wondering how that particular question could have come straight out of left field at him.

"Benito?"

"Yes. Yes, I've heard of them. Hell, I was in them not long ago, investigating a crime. But what—?"

"That's where the rings came from. At least, I think they did. I'm not positive because just before I saw them—"

She stopped mid-sentence, glancing at his hands holding her arms.

Benito realized he'd been tightening his grip and dropped his hands to his sides saying, "Zoe, are you telling me that you saw those rings in the Caves of Balancanchén?"

"Yes. At least, I'm telling you that I think so."

"But you're not certain."

"No. I probably would be if I saw the treasure there again. The jewelry was distinctive, and those rings remind me of some of it, but...why? What difference does it make where they came from?"

"Zoe, it could make a huge difference. It could tell us something really important. About eight months ago, El Gato tried to loot those caves."

"That was the crime you were investigating there?"

"Right. And it was one of the few times things didn't go smoothly for him. The guards discovered him in the lake cavern and almost captured him. He escaped, and only got a few pieces of the treasure. But those few pieces included three rings."

"And you think..." Zoe whispered, her eyes wide.

"Dammit," Benito muttered, trying to force his memory when it didn't want to be forced. "I can't remember the description of the rings he got, but if they're the ones that were in your father's cabin that means El Gato had something to do with hiding them there.''

"But why?"

"I don't know! The man's mind works in convoluted ways. But, Zoe, I have to know if those rings are the ones he stole or not. And you said if you saw the treasure again . . . listen, we can get to the caves in no time. We'll just charter a plane on Cozumel and hop over to the mainland. There's an airstrip at Chichén Itzá, and the caves are only a few miles from . . .''

Zoe was shaking her head. "I can't, Benito," she said. "I can't go into those caves again. It would scare the wits out of me.''

She closed her eyes, not wanting to remember but unable to stop the images flooding her memory.

She was in the caves, following a guide through the tiny, dimly lit passageways. They grew ever narrower and lower, until the two of them had to begin crawling on their hands and knees.

Her throat was growing tighter and her stomach started feeling woozy. The air was damp, heavy with the smell of earth. She wasn't normally claustrophobic but there was something about the caves . . .

The guide sank to his stomach in front of a narrow opening and began wriggling through it like a human snake.

She couldn't do that. As much as she wanted to see the treasure, she couldn't go on, had to go back.

She called out to the guide, telling him that.

"No," he called back, "the exit is at the other end. We do not return the way we came.''

Ahead, more dim lights flashed on, eerily illuminating another stretch of the tiny passage.

"Come," the guide ordered. "I must turn off the lights where you are. There is not so much power to light all the caves at one time."

He'd barely finished speaking before she was plunged into blackness. The only remaining light was the pale wash that spilled through the narrow opening before her. There was no turning back.

Her heart racing, she started forward on her hands and knees. There was nothing she could do but force herself to crawl through that little opening and into the light.

Just as she eased down onto the floor of the cave, she began to hear tiny cries in the darkness surrounding her. Tiny shrill cries and the soft clicks of wings. Fear wrapped itself around her like a shroud. And then—

"Zoe?" Benito said, resting his hands on her arms again and bringing her back to the moment. "Zoe, what the hell's wrong?"

She shook her head, trying to clear it, saying, "There are bats in those caves. Thousands of them. And I was always told that bats never really get tangled in people's hair, that it's just an old wives' tale. But when I was there . . . well, I found out it wasn't. And I was scared spitless, Benito."

Even the recollection made her shiver. The bat had thrashed about, banging against her neck, biting and clawing until she could feel her own hot, sticky blood.

All the while it had been screaming tiny screams that had made her scream as well—until the guide had turned on the lights again, until he'd crawled back to her and untangled the thing from her hair.

After that, they'd continued, but she'd still been shaking when they reached the lake cavern that held the treasure. No wonder she didn't have a perfect recollection of everything she'd seen there.

"Look," she murmured, pushing her hair up off her neck, exposing the tiny white scars that hadn't entirely disappeared. "Bats can be vicious little beasties."

"Oh, Zoe," Benito said, running his fingers softly across the scars.

His touch made her feel warm all over and she looked down, afraid he'd see what she was feeling.

He tucked one finger under her chin and raised her head once more.

"Zoe," he said quietly, his dark eyes not allowing her gaze to leave his, "I understand why you'd never want to go into the caves again. But it's important we know whether those rings are the ones El Gato stole. Important because, if he's got a confederate aboard, he's *definitely* after the *Grifon's* treasure. And with any luck, we can figure out exactly what he's planning and stop him before he can do any harm."

Harm. It was an innocuous-sounding word, but Zoe knew only too well what Benito meant. El Gato had blown Carl's ship out of the water. If he did that to the *Yankee* . . . with her father aboard . . .

"You'd be all right this time," Benito pressed. "You'd be with me."

"Sure," she murmured unhappily. "I'd be with you and a few thousand bats. Benito, there must be another way to identify those rings. Isn't there a description someplace of what was stolen?"

He nodded, saying, "Yeah, I could call headquarters, get someone to check the records. The problem is that El Gato seems to find out so much about things that go on there, I'm certain there's a leak in the department."

"So it's essential I go?" she asked, knowing the answer.

"It really is," Benito said. "But tell you what," he added, gently brushing her hair back from her face. "Before we get to the caves, I'll buy you a scarf to wrap around all this."

His hand lingered on her hair and his eyes lingered on her face. The combination ignited a tiny fire deep within her.

Slowly, she nodded, not sure whether she was agreeing solely because she wanted to help or because helping would mean spending time alone with Benito.

Chapter Eight

Above, a scorching midafternoon sun was beating down. Below, where the sunlight danced and shimmered on the water, Sandy Braukis was tugging on the painter that tied the launch to the *Yankee*—bringing it around to the ladder so he could take Zoe and Benito across to Cozumel's only real city, San Miguel.

Mac glanced at Benito, saying, "What time do you want to be picked up?"

"I don't know when we'll get back from the mainland," Benito told him. "So why don't we play things by ear and call you ship-to-shore."

Mac nodded, then turned to Zoe. "You be careful, baby," he said quietly. "I'm still not convinced your staying aboard is a good idea."

"I won't be aboard, Dad. Not for the rest of today, at least. And I *will* be careful," she promised, although she knew that they were worried about two different things. All *she* could think of was the horrible prospect of being in the Caves of Balancanchén again.

But this time, she was going prepared. Even though it weighed a ton, she had the ship's largest flashlight stashed in her bag. And she'd pulled her hair securely back into a ponytail. And she certainly intended to hold Benito to his offer of buying her a scarf. It was going to be the biggest one she could find, too.

She glanced at him, certain he was prepared, as well. It had to be over ninety degrees. Even the gusting wind was hot. But Benito had on jeans and cowboy boots.

She was sure he'd worn those boots because they gave him a place to conceal his gun. She'd sneaked in and checked her father's desk before coming out on deck, and that little automatic of his hadn't been there.

Finding that out had given her mixed feelings. The fact he thought he might need it made her uneasy, yet she felt reassured knowing he had it.

"Hey, *qué pasa?*" Dean Cooper called, bearing down on them. "So, what are you guys doing?" he asked, reaching Zoe and looking her up and down with those hungry eyes of his.

It made her glad she was wearing cotton pants instead of her customary shorts.

"Just archaeologist stuff," Benito told him. "Thought we'd check out some artifacts."

"Yeah?" Dean said. "Where?"

"We're going to charter a plane and fly over to the mainland."

"Yeah?" Dean repeated.

"There are some caves near Chichén Itzá," Zoe explained. "The Mayans used one of them as a shrine."

"No kidding," Dean said. "Good stuff?"

She nodded, wishing she could think of a way to cut him off without being totally rude. He reminded her of a little kid who was hinting about being invited to a party.

"So... like what kind of good stuff?"

"Well," she said reluctantly, "the main cavern has a lake in it, and people left offerings around it for the rain god."

"No kidding... hey, that sounds like a great place for photographs." He glanced at Mac, saying, "You don't need me around for anything right now, do you? And you guys wouldn't mind my coming along, would you?" he added, looking back at Benito and Zoe.

"It's too dark in the caves to take pictures," Benito said.

"Hell, that's what flash equipment is for," Dean told him. "And I'd be glad to pop for part of what the plane costs. Hey, just let me go grab my camera and stuff, huh? I'll only be a minute."

Without waiting for an answer, Dean turned and started off in the direction of the crew quarters.

Benito quietly muttered a string of obscenities in Spanish. Zoe barely resisted doing the same in English.

Mac just stood there grinning. "Guess you two have got yourselves a chaperon, huh?" he finally said.

It was the first smile Zoe had seen on her father's face all day, and it almost made having to put up with Dean Cooper worthwhile. Almost, but not quite.

BENITO SAT IN THE BACK of the taxi with Zoe, watching the flat stretch of countryside between Chichén Itzá and the Caves of Balancanchén rush past.

Here and there, patches of low jungle growth had been hacked away to make room for tiny adobe houses with tin or thatched roofs, but they were nothing more than passing blurs. The driver was a typical Mexican road warrior.

Suddenly, he slammed on the brakes and they screeched to a halt that practically threw Zoe and Benito onto the floor. Cooper, up front, smacked into the windshield.

"What the hell?" he yelled at the driver, his words barely audible over the cab's blasting horn.

On the road in front of them, a big ugly buzzard nonchalantly glanced up from his road kill.

"Protected species," Benito shouted into Cooper's ear. "You go to jail for killing them. They're like unpaid garbage men."

Finally, the buzzard deigned to flap over to the side of the road and they took off at top speed again.

Zoe glanced at Benito. He simply shook his head, but he knew what she was thinking. They'd gotten this far unscathed, even though the wind had been so strong at the airstrip that their pilot had been hesitant to land. It sure would be ironic if they'd survived that rough landing only to end up in a ditch.

"It's after five," Dean Cooper said, twisting around in the front seat to look back. "You figure these caves are still going to be open?"

"Well, the guides will be gone," Benito said. "But I've met the head guard, so we'll be able to get in."

"Archaeologist privileges, huh?" Copper said.

"Yeah, something like that," Benito told him, trying to decide how to handle things when they arrived.

Getting into the caves wouldn't be any trouble, no matter how late it was. All he had to do was flash his ID at the guards. But he still didn't want his cover blown aboard the *Yankee,* so he had to make sure their photographer didn't learn the real reason they rated special treatment.

Damn but he wished he hadn't let that jerk come along. The way Cooper kept eyeing Zoe made Benito feel like punching him out.

Benito glanced at Zoe and began wishing even more that they were on their own. From the moment she'd agreed to make the trip, all he'd been able to think about was being alone with her—away from all the crazy stuff that had been going on aboard the *Yankee*. But being alone with Zoe and Cooper sure wasn't what he'd had in mind.

Their driver wheeled off the highway and bounced them along the dirt road leading to the caves, then squealed the cab to a stop, raising a cloud of dust that swirled around the car like a minicyclone.

"*¿Hace mucho viento, verdad?*" he said, grinning.

"Yeah, very windy," Cooper muttered. "Good thing we're going to be inside," he added, slinging his gadget bag over his shoulder and opening the door.

Benito arranged for the driver to wait, then joined the others outside the car, saying, "Look, Cooper, I'll see about us getting in. Why don't you take some pictures of Zoe over there in front of the caves?"

"I'm not photogenic," Zoe objected.

"Yeah, well, your father will get a kick out of them," he told her, pretending not to notice her annoyed look.

"Come on, Zoe," Copper said, grabbing her arm.

She shrugged his hand away and marched off toward the caves.

Quickly, Benito located the head guard and explained the situation.

"*Sí*, Señor Cárdenas," the man said. "Myself, I will guide you to the lake cavern. And I will say not a word to anyone."

"I appreciate that, amigo. And we won't take up much of your time. I know the way out, so you can just leave us in the cavern."

They headed over to where Zoe and Cooper were waiting. Zoe was carefully wrapping her new scarf around her head—her new green scarf that Benito had chosen. He'd said it was the exact color of her eyes, and recalling his remark made her smile. Until then, she hadn't been sure he'd even noticed the color of her eyes.

She glanced at the dark hole that was the entrance to the caves and her smile faded. Then, with a deep breath and a tiny prayer, she followed the men out of the sunshine and into the twilight zone inside.

The moment she stepped into the cool dimness, her pulse began racing and her heart started beating erratically. She didn't recall feeling as frightened at the beginning of her first visit, but this time she knew about those bats lurking in the passageways ahead.

The four of them started down the first narrow tunnel in single file—the guard, Dean Cooper, Benito and Zoe bringing up the rear.

She fished the heavy flashlight out of her bag and switched it on, but even with its comforting beam before her, she was having trouble forcing one foot in front of the other. The urge to turn and run began growing stronger with each step.

Then Benito stopped and looked back at her, quietly saying, "You're going to be okay this time. Come on."

He reached out and took her hand, drawing her near. That didn't do anything to slow her pulse. If anything, it seemed to start racing faster yet. But being close to him did make her feel safer.

"You two coming?" Dean Cooper demanded from the shadows ahead.

They continued along, the passageway becoming narrower and lower, until they were crawling forward on their hands and knees.

By the time they reached the tiny opening they had to snake through on their stomachs, and Zoe's heart was beating so loudly she was certain its thudding must be echoing off the walls. But at least that sound was drowning out whatever bat noises there might be.

"You're doing great," Benito said, reaching back again and squeezing her hand. "We're almost there. And when you see the jewelry," he added quietly, "be careful not to say anything Cooper might wonder about."

Ahead of them, Dean Cooper pushed his gadget bag through the hole, then wiggled after it.

"Go on," Benito told her. "Before the guard turns out the lights back here."

Zoe took a deep breath of the cool damp air, screwed up all her courage, and crawled through the opening.

"See?" Benito said, following her. "You did just fine. And the rest of it is a piece of cake."

She managed a smile. But she wasn't taking her scarf off just yet. And she wasn't putting her flashlight away, either.

Benito was right, though. The rest of it *was* a piece of cake. Only a few minutes more walking and they reached the lake cavern.

Benito thanked the guard as he started away.

"*Más tarde,*" Zoe said. "*Y gracias.*"

Dean Cooper didn't seem to even notice the man leaving. He was already busy digging around in his gadget bag.

Zoe switched off her flashlight and stood gazing around the dimly illuminated treasure cave.

Last summer, she'd still been suffering from bat-attack shock when she'd reached the cavern and hadn't fully appreciated its beauty. This time, she slowly drank in the breathtaking picture before her.

The cavern was about sixty feet long and fifty feet across, with lights recessed at irregular intervals along its stone walls. From the cave's ceiling, maybe twenty feet above their heads, stalactites hung like gigantic icicles, many almost reaching the stalagmites that grew upward where the calcite dripped onto the floor. A few had joined into solid pillars.

In the center of the cavern was the underground lake, a beautiful circular pool—deep cerulean blue, but so clear she could see the bottom perfectly. Fish she'd been told were blind swam in the water, and on the far side of it rose a stone image of Tlaloc, the Mayan rain god.

All around the water's edge, and in niches carved into the walls, sat vases and jars. Once, they'd been filled with offerings. Now those treasures were arranged in displays.

Deciding she was safe from the bats in here, Zoe removed her scarf and undid the tight elastic that held her ponytail. Absently, she tucked them into her bag, her gaze wandering over the open displays of treasure. She couldn't remember which of them contained the jewelry that was so much like those three rings.

"Hey," Dean Cooper said, dragging her attention from the artifacts. "Where did that guard guy go?"

Benito told him the guard guy had left. "We only needed him to get us here. The exit is just down that passage," he added, gesturing to the far side of the lake.

"Oh," Dean said. "Well, listen, how about if I take some shots of you two in here?"

Zoe glanced at him doubtfully. She didn't believe he could get half-decent pictures in such poor light. Not even with his flash equipment.

He was probably an okay underwater photographer. Her father wouldn't have him on the *Yankee* otherwise. But she suspected that, on dry land, Dean Cooper was a fish out of water.

She was just about to say she thought taking pictures of them would be a waste of film when Benito said, "Sure, let's get a shot or two."

He strode over to Zoe and draped his arm around her shoulders, drawing her close—making her decide that maybe taking pictures wasn't a waste, after all.

"Why don't you stash that flashlight someplace," he murmured as she fluffed her hair with her free hand. "It won't add much to the shots."

She hid it behind her back while Dean was saying, "No, not there. Stand right in front of the water so I can get that statue thing in the background."

"Rain god," Zoe muttered.

"What?"

"That 'statue thing' is the Mayan rain god."

"Whatever," Dean said as they shifted position. "That's it . . . just a little closer to the water. Good."

He stepped nearer, saying, "I'll start with a close-up. Now, say 'Cheese.'"

Dean's flash exploded, blinding Zoe. Then, while her world was a bright white blur, all hell broke loose.

She sensed Dean Cooper moving forward again. Then Benito was shoving her away from him—so roughly that she lost her balance and stumbled. There was a loud splash and a spray of water hit her.

From behind her Benito was swearing...it must have been him who'd hit the water.

She blinked rapidly, trying to clear her vision. When she succeeded, her eyes froze in horror on Dean Cooper.

He was only a foot away from her, his camera hanging around his neck by its strap, swinging back and forth across his chest.

One of his hands was extended in front of him, the hand that must have pushed Benito into the lake.

And in Dean Cooper's other hand was a gun. A gun trained past Zoe.

Slowly, ever so slowly, she turned. Benito was standing waist-deep in the water. With Dean's gun pointed straight at him.

TIME STOOD STILL...maybe for a minute, maybe for an hour...while Zoe stared, paralyzed, at the two men.

Then her brain revved up to speed and she realized only a few seconds had passed.

Benito took a step forward in the water. Dean Cooper cocked his gun. The sound pierced Zoe's heart.

"What the hell game are you playing at, Cooper?" Benito said, his voice unbelievably calm.

"Sorry, Cárdenas," Dean muttered, "but I'm not playing any game. Your archives folks sent you to the wrong ship at the wrong time, man. I can't have a witness."

His gaze flickered to Zoe for an instant. That was all it took to make her realize exactly what was happening. Dean Cooper was the *someone* who'd been trying to kill her. And now he was going to do it . . . was going to kill not only her, but Benito, as well.

Fear set both her heart and mind racing. She couldn't let that happen.

"First you, Cárdenas," Dean muttered. "Then the captain's daughter."

Suddenly, Zoe was aware of the flashlight—solid and heavy in her hand. She swung it as hard as she could at the gun.

The flashlight smashed down onto Dean's arm and flew out of her grasp.

All in the same second that she hit him, Dean screamed and his gun fired, something clattered to the floor, something splashed into the water. The noise of the shot reverberated around the cavern like deadly thunder.

Mingled with the thunder, Dean Cooper was swearing and Benito was yelling. But everything seemed a single roar of noise to Zoe's ears.

Then Dean Cooper started running—scrambling his way around the end of the lake.

Zoe whirled toward Benito. He was bent down, grabbing at a gun that lay on the bottom of the crystal water. Dean Cooper's gun, her mind said. That's what she'd heard splash.

Benito came up firing at the photographer's running figure . . . again and again. The noise inside the cavern grew deafening.

On the far side of the lake, Dean Cooper ducked behind the statue of Tlaloc, then dashed out from the other side and streaked along the cavern wall.

Benito shot once more, but Dean Cooper was already disappearing down the passage that led to the outside world.

As he vanished, three guards rushed into the cavern, guns drawn, shouting questions. Benito plowed out of the water, explaining things so quickly in Spanish that Zoe could only catch a few words.

He said something about Cooper not stealing any of the treasure . . . merely trying to murder them . . . then he pulled his ID from his jeans and thrust it at the guards.

One look at it and they took off around the end of the lake, in hot pursuit of Dean Cooper.

Zoe stood staring at Benito, her heart in her throat. He'd almost been killed but there he was, alive in front of her.

His clothes were plastered wetly to his body, and he was dripping from head to toe, but what she wanted to do more than anything in the world was throw her arms around him and assure herself he was still in one piece.

He stepped forward and she did exactly that, burying her face against the wet cotton of his shirt.

He hugged her so tightly she could scarcely breathe. She didn't care about breathing, though. All she cared about was his being safe and solid in her arms.

"Nice work, Zoe," he said quietly. "You saved my life."

"What?" She managed to draw back far enough to see his face.

"The flashlight," he said. "By hitting Cooper with the flashlight."

"Oh . . . I did that?" She glanced down, saw it lying on the ground and remembered wielding it.

"Yeah," Benito said, "you did that."

Zoe gazed up at him. She'd saved his life. *She*'d saved his life. "I owed you one," she murmured. "Actually, I owed you two."

"Yeah ... well, thanks."

"De nada," she whispered.

"Sure it was nothing," he said. "Nothing at all, huh?"

"Benito?" she murmured, realizing she was trembling a little. "Why Dean Cooper? He was one of the new crew members. He'd have gotten one of the smallest shares of Dad's estate."

"It would still have been a share in a lot of money," Benito said. "But let's forget about Cooper, huh? Those guards will get him and he'll be in jail till he's old and gray."

Benito stood looking down at her, melting her with his dark eyes. Then, slowly, he bent closer and kissed her ... completing the meltdown.

She pressed her lips to the warmth of his lips, her body to the solid muscles of his body, and kissed him back with every bit of emotion she felt. It was one hell of a lot of emotion.

She started to think about how unbelievable it was that she was standing here kissing Benito when, minutes ago, they'd almost both been killed.

But with him kissing her it proved hard to think about anything except the way his lips tasted ... just a delicious hint of salt ... and the way his tongue was claiming her as his woman ... and the way his hands were moving possessively over her back, molding her body closer and closer to his until they were almost one.

"Zoe," he finally whispered, breaking their kiss. "You could give me a heart attack."

"It's all right, I know CPR," she murmured, wrapping her arms more tightly around his neck and drawing his lips back to hers.

BENITO WOULD HAVE BEEN content to stand in the cave kissing Zoe for eternity, but the head guard arrived, clearing his throat to announce his presence.

Reluctantly, Benito looked over at him, releasing Zoe from his embrace but keeping tight hold of her hands.

"I see you are not harmed, Señor Cárdenas," the guard said, grinning at them. "And my men have told me the treasure is all safe, as well."

"Yes, yes, everything's fine. But what happened to Cooper? Did they get him?"

The guard shook his head, no longer grinning, and said, "I am sorry but no. There was a taxi waiting at the entrance. He raced away in it, and my men, they could not keep up."

"Good God!" Benito snapped, glancing at Zoe. "I was the one who had that taxi waiting for us. First he tries to kill us, then he takes off in *our* taxi. What a helluva nerve."

"Benito, he escaped," Zoe said anxiously, ignoring his attempt to lighten the mood. "He's out there someplace."

"But Zoe, your trouble is over. Now that we know who's been after you, you're safe. Cooper would never dare show his face around the *Yankee* again. And I'll file a report as soon as I can get to a phone. Then every cop in Mexico will be watching for him."

Benito looked over at the guard, saying, "You have a phone in your office?"

"*Sí*, Señor Cárdenas. And my men, one of them will give you a ride to wherever you are going. But the jewels you wanted to see...they told you what you had to know?"

Benito glanced down at Zoe again.

"I didn't get to look at the displays before the excitement started. I'll check now," she said, starting across the cavern.

He started across right along with her. The way she'd been kissing him must have had a peculiar effect on his brain, because he knew he should get on that phone right away, but he couldn't imagine being more than a foot from Zoe.

Actually, even a foot was too far, but it would have to do until they were alone together again.

Zoe gave half a dozen of the displays cursory once-overs, then breathed in sharply and sank to her knees in front of the next one.

"This is it," she murmured. "And oh, Benito, look. There's just no doubt these pieces were made by the same person who made the rings. That's so obvious from the detailing."

He looked. He could see they were similar, but how the hell Zoe knew they were all made by the same person was a mystery to him.

"There's no doubt about it at all, Benito. Those rings came from these caves. And that means..."

She looked up at him, her gaze uneasy. "You said that would mean El Gato is definitely after the *Grifon*'s treasure. And that has to mean my father is in danger, doesn't it?"

Her eyes were asking Benito to say no, to tell her the danger was all over now, but what would be the point in his lying?

She knew she was right about El Gato just as well as she knew she was right about the jewelry.

And she also had to know it wasn't only her father who was in danger from El Gato. It was everyone aboard the *Yankee*.

They might have foiled Dean Cooper's plan, they might have prevented him from murdering Zoe, but the danger was far from over. It was simply wearing a new face.

"We have to get back," Zoe said. "We have to sit down with Dad and figure out exactly what El Gato's up to and what to do about it."

Benito nodded slowly. The last place he wanted to take her was back to that ship, but he could tell she'd go even if she had to swim the entire way.

"Can I use the phone now?" he asked the guard.

"Of course, Señor Cárdenas."

"I'll call the *Yankee* as well as headquarters," he told Zoe. "Let your father know about Cooper. And about the rings. Tell him we're on our way back.

"And that ride you offered," he went on, turning to the guard again. "We're going to need to get to the airstrip in Chichén Itzá."

"You need to fly?" the man said.

"*Sí*, to Cozumel."

"Ahh, no, I think not. The wind, it is getting more strong all the time. The radio, she says there are no more planes landing in the Yucatán tonight. So if no planes land, I think no planes leave."

"Benito . . . what about my father?" Zoe said.

Benito put his hands on her shoulders, saying, "Zoe, nothing will happen on the *Yankee* until after the *Grifon* has been located. When I call, I'll tell Mac to be careful. But El Gato wants that treasure. He'll sit tight until after they've started raising it. At the moment, your father is perfectly safe. I promise."

She nodded slowly. "I guess you're right."

"Maybe you fly to Cozumel mañana," the guard offered. "For tonight, there is a nice hotel near the ruins. Very nice. I call for you if you want."

Benito glanced a question at Zoe.

She gave him a nervous-looking smile and said, "If no planes are flying, then I guess a very nice hotel sounds . . . very nice."

Chapter Nine

Dusk was falling when they reached the Mayaland, but there was still enough light to see that it was, as promised, a very nice hotel.

Zoe thanked the guard who'd driven them, then surveyed the surroundings while Benito tipped the man.

The main building was old colonial, with soft light spilling from its lobby and elegant dining room. Lighted paths crisscrossed the jungle garden setting, leading to little thatch-roofed guest bungalows, each with its own tiny porch and welcoming light over the door.

The property was surprisingly sheltered from the strong winds. Palm fronds rustled above, but there was nothing ominous about the sound.

Nearer ground level, the flowering shrubs were almost still. They merely whispered softly in the gathering night. The sounds of insects, the sweet fragrances in the air, made Zoe wish things could always be as peaceful.

Wishing didn't make it so, though. She was extremely aware of Benito's gun in her bag. He'd taken it out of his wet boot and asked her to carry it, and having it was a constant reminder they still had El Gato to worry about.

But he wasn't an immediate threat. Whoever and wherever El Gato actually was, Benito had to be right. Nothing would happen before they'd started to raise the *Grifon*'s treasure.

So, for tonight, she was going to pretend they were in a world with no problems, no worries, no dangers.

She heard the car leaving and turned to Benito.

Simply looking at him made her smile. Even though the circumstances of their meeting had been crazy, she'd fallen so very much in love with him.

And she knew he'd fallen in love with her. Neither of them had spoken the words, but what difference could three little words possibly make?

She couldn't resist touching him—brushed her hand across his shirt, saying, "Your clothes are still wet. And mine are a mess from those tunnels. That dining room looks too classy for us."

"Well, we could think about room service," he said slowly.

"Think about room service...you know, I think room service sounds perfect."

That made him smile, but he seemed a little uncertain. "Zoe," he said, "before we go in to register..."

"Yes?"

"Look, I'm certain Dean Cooper is going to try to get a million miles away from Mexico, as fast as he can. But just in case...well, there's no way I could even think about leaving you alone tonight, so when I called from the caves I only reserved one bungalow. But I'll make sure it has two beds. I mean, I'm not assuming..."

She reached out and took his hand, loving him all the more because he wasn't assuming. "Maybe," she murmured, "you could ask the desk clerk about a double bed. I'll wait out here while you register."

"Zoe..." He didn't finish the sentence, just leaned closer and kissed her before starting for the lobby.

Watching him stride away, she began thinking that he was the only person who'd ever saved her life. He'd saved her life and she'd saved his. And wasn't there a cosmic rule about that binding two people's karmas together forever?

Not that there actually *was* any possible forever with Benito. Come September, she'd be back in California. And he'd be gone even before that—as soon as the trouble with El Gato was sorted out. But right now he was with her and she loved him.

She stood gazing into the twilight until Benito came back out of the lobby and headed across to her.

A warm swirl of anticipation began curling through her body. By the time they were inside their bungalow, the little swirl had become such a hot rush of desire she could scarcely take her eyes off Benito.

Then she saw the bed and could scarcely take her eyes off it. It was straight out of a fairy tale—draped with a white cloud of mosquito netting that flowed from the ceiling to the floor. A braided cord, looped over the bedpost, drew back a section of fabric to provide an opening.

Forcing her gaze from the bed, she glanced around the rest of the small room.

Its walls were pristine white, the floor terra-cotta tiles. Above, attached to a beam stretching beneath the thatched roof, a ceiling fan lazily turned.

She moved closer to the bed and put her bag on the small table beside it, while Benito shut the door.

He hadn't turned on the inside light, and when the wash of light from the porch disappeared, all that was left was a faint glow straying in through the window, providing just enough illumination to let her see that he was looking at her with undisguised longing.

He crossed the few steps between them, then softly brushed her hair back from her face, his fingers leaving warmth where they touched.

"What do you think?" he said quietly. "Should I see about that room service right now?"

"What I think," she murmured, "is that you should see about taking off those wet clothes right now."

"Ahh . . . I don't have anything to change into, you know."

"I know."

The corners of his mouth turned upward, into the sexiest smile she'd ever seen. She didn't have much chance to enjoy looking at it, though. A second later, he put his arms around her, drew her close and kissed her.

She shivered, not because of his wet clothes against her, but because of his body against hers, hard and male and making her want him.

He began caressing the inside of her lips with his tongue, then kissed her with such devastating thoroughness that she moaned, pressing even closer to him, her body wanting the delight of his kisses everywhere.

"Zoe?" he whispered, relaxing his hold.

She clung to him more tightly.

Firmly, he took her by the shoulders and stepped back from her, saying, "Zoe, give me my gun."

Uncertainly, she reached for her bag, dug inside it, and withdrew the little automatic.

He slid it under one of the pillows, then turned back to her. "Like I said, I'm sure Cooper's a hundred miles away, but let's not take any chances."

She swallowed hard, not wanting to think there could be danger lurking in the darkness outside. Then Benito wrapped his arms around her, kissing her again, and she couldn't think of anything but him.

His fingers slipped to her blouse and he began unbuttoning it, his dark eyes watching her. He eased the thin fabric off her shoulders and smoothed his hands across the scrap of lace that was her bra. It did almost nothing to conceal her breasts... absolutely nothing to conceal the way her nipples were hard and straining for his touch.

He caressed them, making them ache for more, while he began a trail of kisses down her throat that started a throbbing need deep within her.

When his trail reached her breasts, when he covered one nipple with his mouth and kissed it through the silky lace, she began to quiver.

"Let's get rid of this," he murmured, pushing the lace up, leaving her breasts entirely naked to his lips.

She pressed her lower body against his, whispering, "Hey, you're the one who's supposed to be getting undressed."

He drew back a little, lightly stroking her nipples with his thumbs, and smiled that sexy smile once more. "Anyone ever tell you you're a pushy woman, Zoe MacLeish?"

"Almost everyone I've ever met," she murmured, unbuttoning his shirt.

His sharp intake of breath, when she slipped his shirt open by smoothing her hands across his naked chest, made her glad she was pushy.

"But no one's ever taken me to bed under mosquito netting before," she hinted.

"No?"

"No." She slid her fingers down over the zipper of his jeans.

He covered her hands with his own, pressing hers against the rock hardness of his erection.

Touching him like that made her want him all the more, and she fumbled with the button on his waistband, having trouble because the denim was wet, but finally getting it undone.

"Wait a minute," Benito said, taking her hands in his. "I want to tell you something first. Zoe . . . I love you."

His words hung in the air between them, and if there was anything she could have done to keep them from escaping into the night, she'd have done it.

Those three little words *did* make a difference, after all. But they only made a difference because it was Benito who had said them to her.

"I love you, too," she murmured.

He slowly exhaled, as if he'd actually thought there was some doubt about that. Then he picked her up in his arms, so easily she might have weighed nothing.

"What?" she said, laughing. "What are you doing?" But she knew exactly what he was doing and kicked off her shoes as he carried her the few feet to the bed.

"Zoe, if no one's ever taken you to bed under mosquito netting before, I'd better make it special."

"Oh, Benito, do you really think there's a chance it won't be?"

"Well," he told her with a grin, "there's a trick to this." He reached though the opening and tugged down the top sheet. "See, you don't want to get all tangled up in this netting," he explained, easing her onto the bed.

He yanked off his boots, disposed of the rest of their clothes in less than a second and climbed in after her— all beautiful bronze male, clearly as aroused by her as she was by him.

"And you want privacy from insects," he said, releasing the cord that held part of the netting back.

The opening closed. A heavily gathered, filmy curtain totally surrounded the bed.

"And what else do I want?" Zoe whispered, her entire body hot with desire.

Benito propped himself up on one elbow and looked at her in the dimness. "You want me to touch you," he said, sinking his fingers into the thickness of her hair.

He cupped the back of her head with his hand, so she was gazing into the depths of his eyes. They were full of love and care and longing.

"Zoe," he murmured, more tenderly than she'd ever heard her name spoken. Then, slowly, he traced a line from her temples to her lips, on down her throat to her breast.

"And you want me to kiss you," he said, leaning over her more closely, his mouth following the line downward, exciting her impossibly more now that she was naked.

His hand moved lower... to her hip... to her inner thigh... teasing... ever nearer to where she was throbbing for his touch... but he held back.

"Mmm," she murmured, running her fingers across his chest, brushing the hardness of his nipples, then sliding her hands down over his stomach, reaching to hold him as intimately as she could.

"Oh, Zoe," he whispered when she circled him and started to caress the length of his hardness.

Finally, he slipped his hand between her legs, making her moan with relief. Then he began his own gentle, rhythmic caress, his touch turning her liquid with desire.

Each slow stroke made her breathe faster. Each passing moment made her breathing more ragged. Each time he whispered how crazy she was making him feel, she wanted him more.

"Benito," she whispered. "Benito, you're making me crazy, too."

He moved over her then, hot skin against hot skin, setting her completely afire, exciting her so she could barely breathe at all, his heaviness pinning her so she could barely move... but she had to move. He was making her body respond in an age-old rhythm that couldn't be stilled.

He kissed her with a long, passionate, searching kiss, then eased lower, kissing her throat, her breasts, her stomach, still driving her mad with his hands, until he drove her completely out of control and her body took over from her mind.

She climaxed in a series of shudders, an erotic torment of pleasure, arching against his hand again and again, knowing she was going to scream if he kept touching her the way he was, knowing she was going to scream if he stopped.

Vaguely, she was aware of making animal noises deep in her throat, of saying his name over and over again. And then his name disintegrated into a string of tiny moans while she tried to catch even a slight breath.

Slowly, gradually, her body began to grow satiated with the delicious torture of his touch. Eventually, the tremors that had seized her began to subside.

Still breathless, she sank against the pillow, saying something she knew couldn't make sense to Benito because it didn't to her.

He lay on top of her, not moving until she felt another stirring of arousal begin to throb inside her.

She reached for him again, this time guiding him, still rock hard, into her.

"Oh, Zoe," he whispered, "you feel so good."

"Mmm," she murmured, "from this side, too."

He began moving gently back and forth, fitting himself perfectly to her, then, with a moan, began to drive harder and faster, making her breathing ragged again, carrying her closer and closer to the brink of another orgasm.

Just as her body exploded into a fresh series of shivering spasms, she felt him shuddering against her... and was aware once more how very special she felt with him.

A minute later he collapsed on top of her, his weight heavy, but she wouldn't have tried to move for the world.

Eventually, he eased onto his side, tucking the sheet around her sweat-slick body and cuddling her silently against him.

"Zoe?" he finally murmured, after they'd lain together for so long the room had grown completely black. "Zoe? You're smiling."

"Uh-huh," she said, wondering how he could tell. Then she realized he was brushing her lips with his fingertips—so gently she could scarcely feel them.

Covering his hand with hers, she began kissing his fingers, each one in turn. "You could make me stop smiling," she whispered. "All you'd have to do is nail down the corners of my mouth."

He laughed...and what could possibly be better than a man who laughed at her jokes? It started her thinking once more about how much she loved him.

That was all she thought about...and dreamed about...the entire night.

WHEN THE BRIGHT FINGERS of morning crept into the bungalow and woke Zoe, she was lying in Benito's arms. She gave him a lazy smile, then a not-so-lazy kiss.

"You know what?" he said as she snuggled against his chest.

"You're starving?" she guessed. Not that missing dinner last night hadn't been worth it, but he had to be as hungry now as she was.

"Well, yeah, but that wasn't what I was going to say. I've been lying here considering things."

"Uh-huh?"

"And...well, now that Dean Cooper is out of the picture...I mean, now that there's nobody trying to kill you...well, I've been thinking it would make sense for you to go back to California for a few weeks."

"What?" she said, easing up into a sitting position and eyeing Benito uncertainly.

He crossed his arms behind his head and stared at the mosquito netting above, saying, "See, what I was thinking is that even if Cooper doesn't get picked up right away, he sure isn't still part of your father's crew. So he no longer has a reason to try to kill you. That means you'd be safe back in your apartment and—"

"Just hold on a minute," she interrupted, pulling the sheet up around her neck. What the hell was going on here? Benito sounded as if he wanted to get rid of her.

"Benito, let me get this straight. Until yesterday, there was a guy on the *Yankee* who was out to murder me. But there I was, aboard ship. And now you're saying that since he's gone, since I'm not in danger anymore, I should leave? What the hell kind of logic is that?"

"Dammit," he said, sitting up and giving her a look that smacked of righteous indignation. "This has nothing to do with Cooper. It—"

"No?" she demanded. "Well, what does it have to do with?"

"El Gato."

"El Gato," she repeated.

"Exactly. You may not be in danger from Cooper any longer, but there's still El Gato."

"He's after the treasure, not me."

"Right. But he's never been concerned about anyone who gets in his way. So I want you out of his way, okay?"

"No, Benito, it sure as hell is *not* okay. And who do you think you are, trying to order me around?"

"I think I'm the man who loves you, dammit!"

"What? You love me, so you want to hustle me off and never see me again? What kind of loving me is that?"

"Who said anything about never seeing you again? I'm just telling you that, until I've caught El Gato, you should leave. That doesn't mean I don't love you."

"Oh? Well, if you love me, why are you sitting there yelling at me?"

"Dammit, Zoe, I'm not yelling. And I love you like crazy."

"I see. Then maybe you could stop being so damned bossy. Pushy women don't like being bossed."

"Zoe, this is for your own good."

That one started her sizzling. "Pushy women," she snapped, "*really* don't like being told to do something because it's for their own good. You listen to me, Benito Cárdenas. If you think I'm running back to California when my father has big trouble on his hands, you've got another think coming."

"Oh? Well, you listen to me, Zoe MacLeish. We'll just see about that. When we get back to the *Yankee*, I intend to tell your father I think you'd be safer somewhere else."

"You wouldn't dare."

"I sure as hell *would* dare. It's for your own damned good."

He'd said it again. That got her so mad she couldn't come up with a response, so she grabbed the mosquito netting and tried to find the opening in its voluminous gathers.

"How the hell do I get out of this stupid bed?" she finally yelled. "And keep away from me," she ordered when Benito pressed his naked body against her from behind.

"You want me to let you out of here or not? There," he shouted, his voice almost drowning out the sound of the net ripping. "You're out."

She shoved the shredded edges of the fabric apart and threw her legs over the side of the bed, smacking her feet noisily on the cold tiles.

Then she grabbed the tangle of her clothes from the floor, used them to hide her bare behind as best she could, and stomped across the room to the bathroom—so angry she was muttering to herself.

She'd made dumb mistakes before, but none of them had even been in the same league as actually thinking she'd fallen in love with that arrogant, bossy, Señor Thinks-He-Knows-Everything Cárdenas.

THEY'D EATEN BREAKFAST at the Mayaland in frosty silence. They'd flown from Chichén Itzá to Cozumel in an atmosphere that would have frozen hell over. And Zoe was certain their icy glares had set Sandy Braukis shivering when they were coming out to the *Yankee*.

But that hadn't stopped Benito from starting in on her father about her going home, the minute they'd stepped onto the deck.

If he hadn't taken his darned gun back, she'd have shot him by now. As it was, if he trotted out just one more reason why she should leave, she intended to head to her father's cabin, get the Colt from his desk, and shoot Señor Cárdenas in the...well, making love under mosquito netting, or anywhere else, wouldn't be one of his future options.

"Benito is right, Zoe," Mac said. "There's no point in taking chances, so I want you to go home. Once this is over, you can come back for the rest of the summer, okay?''

"No," she said.

Benito made a conscious effort to unclench his jaw. That woman was so damned stubborn he'd like to tie her to a mule and send her home that way.

"What do you mean, no?" Mac asked her.

"You asked me if it was okay, and I said no, it's not okay. I'm not going home."

"Baby—"

"No. Just listen to *me* instead of to that...that Benito."

She'd said his name as if it was a dirty word, so he gave her a black look. It seemed to make no impression whatsoever. She just went on talking to Mac.

"Dad, you *might* have convinced me to leave when Dean Cooper was still playing kill-the-captain's-daughter, but you're not convincing me now. My research is what started your search for the *Grifon*, remember?"

"Of course I remember, but—"

"Plus, you're suddenly missing a photographer and I don't take bad shots—neither of wreck sites nor of raised artifacts. I'm at least good enough to satisfy the government."

"Zoe—"

"Dad, I'm not leaving simply because you and Benito are paranoid about what El Gato is up to. I swear, if you throw me off the *Yankee*, I'll rent a room on Cozumel and see if *I* can find out who he is and what he's up to."

"Dammit, Zoe!" Benito said. "That's *all* we'd need. *You* playing detective."

"Oh? Well let's not forget that *I'm* the one who recognized those rings. So I'm hardly a total washout as a detective."

"Listen," Mac said, eyeing Benito, "I haven't had a chance to tell you about these, but Zoe's just reminded me about them. Look."

He reached into his pocket and drew out a pair of etched gold earrings, saying, "After you called last night, I searched through Cooper's things and came up with these. Maybe it's a long shot, but you think they might be something else El Gato stole? Like the rings?"

Benito stared at them, not knowing *what* to think. There *had* been a pair of gold earrings taken from Balancanchén, along with the rings. But he didn't have a clue whether these might be the ones or not. He couldn't even tell whether they were actually old or reproductions. Reluctantly, he glanced at Zoe.

She was staring studiously out across the water.

He cleared his throat.

She ignored him—stubborn as that mule he'd like to tie her to.

"Zoe..." Mac said in a menacing tone.

Her father rated a glance, accompanied by an infuriatingly innocent, "Yes?"

"Zoe, stop playing games. Have a look at these damned things and tell us what you think."

"Me?" she said, pretending to be shocked. "You two big, strong, intelligent men need help from *me?*"

"Dammit, Zoe..." Benito muttered.

"I'll tell you what," she offered with a sweet smile. "If you're both sure I've heard the last of any talk about sending me packing, I'd be glad to help."

"That's blackmail," Benito snapped.

Zoe shrugged and looked out over the water again.

Mac shook his head as if he could cheerfully strangle her, finally saying, "You just *are* stubborn enough to get a room on Cozumel if I say you can't stay aboard, aren't you?"

"Yes, I just am."

"Zoe, sometimes you make me so mad I want to... All right. You can stay. So tell us about these earrings."

She flashed Benito a triumphant glance that made him see red, and reached for the earrings.

"Uh-huh," she said, tracing one of them with a finger.

"Uh-huh, what?" he demanded.

"Uh-huh, they're from Balancanchén. From the same collection as the rings."

"Which means?" Mac asked, looking at Benito.

"Which means . . ." he said slowly, trying to figure out what the hell it *did* mean. "Which means there's a connection between El Gato and Dean Cooper."

"You're saying Cooper could actually *be* El Gato."

"No, that isn't it, Mac. I checked out your crew carefully and none of them could be El Gato. It has to be that Cooper was working for El Gato."

"Ben, what the hell? You swore up and down that El Gato wasn't behind trying to kill Zoe."

"And I'm still sure he wasn't. Cooper must have been playing two games at once—trying to kill Zoe on his own, looking to get a share of your estate, and also working for El Gato. So it would have been Cooper who stashed those rings in your cabin."

"But why?" Zoe said.

Benito looked at her with annoyance. Bad enough she'd gotten her own way about staying. He could certainly live without her asking questions he hadn't yet figured out the answers to.

"Well?" she pressed.

He stood rubbing his jaw while the pieces started falling into place. "Dammit, but El Gato is good," he admitted grudgingly.

"You want to elaborate on that?" Mac asked.

"Mac, back when Billy Bird showed up with the first ring, and Zoe said it was so valuable, I started to wonder... you're not going to like this, but I started to think you were into something illegal."

"What?" Mac roared.

"I told you you weren't going to like it. But what the hell was I supposed to think? And you know, that was exactly what I *was* supposed to think, what El Gato wanted me to think. Hell, I haven't fooled him at all. He knows who I really am, probably has all along. There I was, worrying about what would happen if he found out, and he knew all along."

"I'm not following this," Zoe put in.

"It would be just like him," Benito muttered. "He thinks he's so damned much smarter than the *federales,* it would be just like him."

"For God's sake," Mac snapped. "What would be just like him?"

"Finding out right at the start that I'm not a government archaeologist, finding out I'm really the one who's been after him all this time, then trying to use me to his advantage. See, he had Cooper plant those stolen rings in your cabin to try to incriminate you. Cooper probably told him how Billy was always playing around with your stuff. And El Gato figured I'd..."

"You'd what?" Mac said.

"Well, before I decided you really hadn't known anything about those rings, I was considering arresting you."

"What!"

"Mac, it's my job. If I'd believed you were stealing valuable artifacts, I'd have had you thrown in jail. And that would have put you out of the picture, out of El Gato's road...made things easier for him. But as it's turned out, you aren't out of the picture and his friend Cooper is."

"Maybe El Gato will give up, then," Zoe said, looking hopeful. "With things not going his way, maybe he'll give up on his plot."

Benito shook his head, saying, "I doubt it. The more I see how much effort he's put into this plan, the less I think he'll just give up. He figures things not going his way is a challenge, so he'll still be around, watching and waiting."

"We'd better keep on being damned careful, then," Mac said.

"Yeah, we'd sure better." Benito stood gazing at Zoe. With her stubbornness, he was going to have to keep on being damned careful for both of them.

Watching her, he suddenly started thinking about the way she'd looked this morning angrily marching away from the bed, unsuccessfully trying to cover herself with that ridiculous pile of clothes. The image almost made him laugh, and banished the last trace of his anger.

Infuriating as she was, he had a feeling he'd never be able to stay mad at Zoe MacLeish for long. And surprisingly enough, she seemed to have cooled down as much as he had. Hell, a few more minutes and she might even smile at him.

He still wished she'd agreed to go home where she'd be safe, though. Then, after this was over . . . well, he didn't know exactly what would happen then. He only knew that, as furious as she could make him, he wanted *something* to happen after this was over.

But first, he had to make sure they all got through this alive.

Chapter Ten

A sultry night breeze that smelled of the sea wafted across the *Yankee*'s deck. It was nothing at all like the near hurricane that had kept Benito and Zoe on the mainland last night, yet last night was exactly what it was making her think of. But then, all day long, *everything* had been making her think about last night.

She glanced surreptitiously at Benito, stretched out on the lounge chair beside hers. She wasn't surreptitious enough, though. He caught her looking and gave her a slow, sexy smile.

Even in the moonlight, it practically melted her, so she quickly looked away.

They'd called a truce in the war that had erupted between them this morning. After all, they had to work together if they were going to trap El Gato. But a truce didn't mean she intended to sleep with the enemy again. Not ever.

She'd made a mistake last night. Repeating it would be moronic. Their fight had made her realize they were as incompatible as two people could possibly be.

Actually, she'd known that from the moment they'd met, but somehow she'd let herself think...well, she'd only *thought* she was in love with Benito. And she'd thought wrong. Even setting aside his Spanish macho arrogance, his bossiness and his hundred other dislikable traits...

He reached over and took her hand. She swallowed hard, knowing she should draw it away but unable to move a muscle. There were a few things about Benito she found impossible to dislike, and the way his touch made her feel so warm inside was one of them.

"Zoe?"

The deep timbre of his voice saying her name was another. She just hoped he didn't manage to string too many of those impossible-to-dislike things together.

"Zoe," he said again, "are you going to feel okay on your own tonight?"

She glanced at him, trying to see his expression clearly in the moonlight. It was impossible. All she could see were the chiseled planes and angles of his face, but that was enough to start a hollow ache in her chest, suspiciously close to her heart. "What do you mean by feel okay?" she managed.

"I mean...hell, Zoe, I mean I'm going to be worried sick if I'm way down aft in the crew quarters and you're in your cabin alone."

The time had definitely come to remove her hand from his. She did, saying, "Benito, Dad and I agreed you were right—odds are there won't be any trouble aboard before we locate the *Grifon*. And I won't be in my cabin alone. Billy Bird will be with me."

Benito took her hand again, this time so firmly that pulling it away would be difficult. "All right," he said. "I just figured maybe...I remember Mac saying he sleeps sounder than a dead man, but I guess it would be too awkward, with his cabin right across from yours... hell, maybe I could just camp outside your door or something, huh?''

''No,'' she murmured. ''It's not the awkwardness. Not entirely. I just don't want to... well, you know.''

''No, dammit, I don't know. I don't understand what the hell is going on here. So maybe we had a minor disagreement. But Zoe, I meant every word I said last night. I love you. That wasn't just talk. I love you and I don't want anything to happen to you.''

She stared down at the deck, telling her pulse to stop racing and her heart to stop pounding. She didn't *want* Benito to love her and she didn't want to love him.

She did love him, of course. She could deny it all she wanted, but deep down she'd still known she loved him.

If she grew to love him more, though... well, nothing could ever possibly work out between them in the long run. And a little hurt now had to be better than the enormous hurt she'd feel if she let herself love him more.

''Benito,'' she murmured, ''I'll be fine tonight. Really. And I think it would be best...'' She couldn't go on. Tears were welling up in her eyes, and her throat hurt so badly she couldn't say another word, so she simply pushed herself off the lounger and ran to her cabin.

She'd half expected him to follow, and when he didn't she felt both better and worse. If he had, if he'd taken her in his arms and... but it was just as well he hadn't.

Miserably, she leaned against the door, telling herself not to cry, then flicked on the light, carefully locked the door and wiped her eyes.

When she finally turned around, Billy Bird strutted along his perch, saying "Hi, Zoe, I've missed you."

"Oh, Billy," she said, her throat still aching with tears. "What do you think? Do you think I'm an idiot? Do you think I'm making a terrible mistake?"

"Hi, Zoe, I've missed you," he repeated their usual greeting.

"Hi, Billy Bird," she whispered. "I've missed you, too."

She got ready for bed, trying unsuccessfully to stop thinking about Benito. But even after she'd turned out the light and crawled into her berth, she could think of nothing else.

Fiercely, she hugged the pillow, telling herself she didn't really wish he was with her now, telling herself to go to sleep—that everything would seem better in the morning.

After an eternity of tossing and turning, she drifted into a state between sleeping and waking, fraught with weird nightmares and shapeless black forms.

Several times she jolted awake. Sometimes certain she was falling through darkness to her death. Sometimes certain there was a person lurking in the cabin, about to leap out of the shadows at her.

She'd almost decided to give up trying to sleep and read for a while—anything except a murder mystery—when she dozed off again.

The next time she jerked awake she was drenched in sweat and it was much later. The moon had drifted far enough across the sky to have entirely changed the pattern of black shapes in her cabin.

She eyed each of them in turn, focusing on them one by one until she was able to determine what it really was. Her locker . . . a chair . . . the pile of clothes she'd peeled off earlier and left in a heap on the floor.

Her gaze moved on to the next one, the hump near the foot of her berth. That one was . . . her mind drew a blank.

The longer she tried to think of what it could be, the more frightened she grew. The more frightened she grew, the more annoyed with herself she became.

"This is ridiculous," she finally muttered, sitting up and reaching for the light.

That was when the shape lunged at her.

She tried to scream; her throat was frozen with fear.

The solid shadow grabbed her pillow and pushed it over her face, forcing her head back onto the mattress.

She struggled, but the pillow was pressing harder and harder against her, making it impossible to breathe.

And then Billy Bird started shrieking. A man yelped sharply. Billy screeched again. Another pained yell. Then the cabin was alive with screeches and cries, until suddenly there was no pressure pushing the pillow against her.

Zoe shoved it off her face. She reached for the light once more but didn't need it.

Her cabin door flew open. Light streamed in from the passageway, almost blinding her. All she could see was the dark shape of a man hurtling out through the doorway. Then all she could hear was the thud of footsteps running down the passageway.

BENITO DRAGGED HIMSELF from the depths of sleep, uncertain where he was. He brushed his hand over what he was lying on, trying to identify it. Lounge chair...lounge chair he'd moved along the deck so he could spend the night near Zoe's cabin. But he hadn't meant to fall asleep.

His mind instantly grew alert. A noise had wakened him. He listened for a second, then sprang to his feet.

Someone was running along the deck. In the middle of the night, someone was running along the deck—away from the bow, heading for the stern.

He raced to the passageway that led to the fore cabins. The moment he wheeled in from the deck he could see that Zoe's door was standing open, her light was on.

Fear twisted his gut and he tore into her cabin full tilt, terrified that...

She was all right. He stopped and stood staring at her, immobilized with relief. Whatever had happened, she was all right, was standing beside her berth, wearing a clinging white nightshirt.

Then he realized her face was almost as pale as the shirt, noticed she was trembling.

She didn't say a word, merely crossed the few feet between them, wrapped her arms around him and hugged him as if she'd never let him go.

"Zoe," he murmured. She was soft and warm and alive in his arms, and he hugged her back so tightly he was afraid she might break. "Zoe, what happened?"

"A man," she whispered. "I woke up and a man was in my cabin. Benito, I remembered to lock it but he got in and...and he tried to smother me."

"Oh, God! Zoe, do you know who it was?"

She shook her head against his chest, saying, "I couldn't see."

"Zoe, I have to go after him. If I don't catch him right now we won't know who it was."

"We'll know," she murmured, loosening her hold and gazing up at him. "I'm sure we'll know. Look." She gestured at Billy Bird, sitting quietly on his perch.

"What?"

"Benito, look at his claws."

He looked. They were smeared with wet blood.

"Good God," he said, drawing Zoe close again. "I'd never have believed I'd have a good word to say about that bird. But first chance I get, I'm going to buy him a lifetime supply of crackers."

"Crackers?" Billy said.

"He likes that idea," Zoe whispered, almost smiling, then pressing her cheek against Benito's chest once more.

He rested his chin on the top of her head, breathing in the fresh scent of spring from her hair.

When she'd finally stopped shaking, he said, "Let's go wake your father. You can stay with him while I find whoever was in here."

They pounded on Mac's door—he really *did* sleep sounder than a dead man—then quickly explained what had happened.

Mac turned white under his tan—almost as white as Zoe had been. He grabbed for his clothes, muttering, "I'll kill the bastard."

"No," Benito said. "We shouldn't leave Zoe sitting here alone. And if anyone's going to kill the bastard, it's going to be me."

He left Zoe in Mac's arms, his urge to kill so strong it scared him. Pulling his automatic from the special pocket in his shorts, he headed rapidly down the deck.

Above, on the observation platform, the lanky figure of Jake was silhouetted in the moonlight. Fat lot of good he'd been, standing watch. Hell, given the way he was leaning against the railing, he was probably asleep.

Or maybe that was an act. Maybe it was he who'd...

Pausing, Benito considered his options. He could start by checking on Jake...but no, he'd start with the crew cabins. If anyone was missing, he'd know who he was after. And if someone was in his quarters and bleeding...that urge to kill got even stronger.

He tried the senior crew quarters first—threw open the door, flicked on the light...and was greeted by a chorus of muttered obscenities.

His quick bed check found Chicken, Sandy Braukis and Marco Vinelli—all in their berths, all glaring at him through sleepy eyes, all apparently untouched by Billy Bird.

"Sorry, I'll explain in the morning," Benito told them, switching the light off again. He pulled the door closed and stepped across to his own cabin.

With Dean Cooper gone and Jake up top, there should be Danny Doyle and Sam Johnson inside. This time, turning on the light told him what he wanted to know.

Only Danny Doyle started muttering angrily. Sam Johnson wasn't there.

"Sorry," Benito said. He flicked off the light, pulled the door closed, and started back for the deck at a run.

He reached it and stopped, trying to figure where Sam would have gone. Since he was a diver...hell, maybe he'd grab some gear and try to swim to Cozumel.

Benito was just turning to head for the equipment room when he heard a soft scraping noise on the *Yankee*'s hull, barely audible above the lapping waves.

Looking over at the rail, he saw the gate was open. He rushed across and peered down. Just visible at the bottom of the ladder, sketchily outlined by the moonlight, was a dark figure—pulling on the painter that tied the launch to the ship.

Hell, Sam was going to try to make Cozumel, all right, but he wasn't intending to swim.

"Sam," he shouted. "Sam, give it up."

Looking down to the black water, he couldn't see what effect his words had. Then a moonbeam caught a tiny glint of silver and he dived for the deck.

A shot exploded. A bullet whizzed over his head.

He grabbed his gun from his pocket and crawled to the rail. "Shoot again and I'll kill you, Sam," he yelled.

Another shot blasted into the night. Again, the bullet came so close he could hear it cut the air.

Heart thudding, he snaked forward a couple of inches, reaching his forearm over the edge and firing toward the bottom of the ladder.

The roar of his own bullet in his ear... silence below... then a splash. Had he hit Sam? Or had the man decided that clinging to the ladder made him an easy target?

Benito edged even closer to the gate opening and peered down.

For a moment he could see nothing but black water, broken only by the moonlight glistening on the surface. Then he made out a head... an arm slicing through the water. Sam was swimming to the *Yankee*'s stern—heading for the launch.

Scrambling to his feet, Benito shoved his gun back into its special pocket. He kicked off his sneakers, then dove from the deck into the dark water of the Caribbean.

Pushing with all his strength, he surged back to the surface. Sam was already hauling himself over the side of the launch.

Benito began swimming as hard as he could, hoping to hell Sam didn't turn around and start shooting again.

He didn't. Maybe he'd lost his gun to the sea because he raced for the steering wheel without a backward glance.

But he'd need a key to start the boat and . . .

Suddenly Benito remembered Zoe saying that Mac kept a spare key in the glove compartment. Maybe Sam didn't know that, though. Maybe . . .

The launch's motor came alive with a throaty roar.

From the observation platform, Jake the Rake had started yelling. But he was too late. Sam was working on the rope, trying to untie the motorboat from the *Yankee*.

It was a race now, between Sam's freeing that boat and Benito's reaching it.

Then his fingers touched its hull. He'd made it. He grabbed the side with both hands and pulled himself up and over, landing in a crouch on the floor of the boat.

Sam whirled around, shoving his hand into his pants as he turned.

Benito's brain jolted into overdrive. Sam hadn't lost his gun at all, and they'd just reached final show time.

Benito pushed up from his crouch and heaved himself through the air, seeing the gun appear in Sam's hand just as he smashed into the man.

The impact sent them both down, sprawling over the boat's bench seat. Benito grabbed for Sam's arm. Came up empty. Scrambled to his feet in the wildly rocking boat...and found himself staring into the barrel of the gun.

"Sam!" Zoe screamed from the deck above them.

For one split second, the man's gaze wavered. In that split second, Benito kicked Sam's arm with all his force. Sam shrieked like a wounded animal.

Benito threw himself at the diver, pinning him to the floor.

He wrestled one of Sam's arms down, then slammed the other against the seat—so hard he'd have known he'd broken it even without Sam's agonized scream.

A glance to either side assured him the gun was gone, lost in the scuffle, and he focused on Sam's moonlit face.

It was contorted in pain. And Billy Bird had done quite a job on it. Both of the diver's cheeks had been raked raw and there was a wound on his neck that was oozing blood.

Benito jammed one knee into Sam's gut, saying, "Let's have it. Why did you try to kill Zoe?"

ZOE WATCHED HER FATHER pace the breadth of his cabin once more, raking his fingers through his hair.

He kept looking over to his berth, where she was sitting with Benito, then back at Sam Johnson, but he hadn't started his interrogation yet.

Even though Benito had gotten the basic story and filled them in, Mac had insisted he was going to hear every last detail from Sam. And Zoe was darned interested in hearing what their Al Pacino look-alike had to say, too.

Sam, though, clearly wasn't looking forward to talking. In fact, sitting in that chair, holding his broken arm with his good one, he looked as if he'd rather be anyplace else on earth.

Between the damage Billy had inflicted and what Benito had done, she almost felt sorry for Sam. Almost, but not quite. He'd tried to kill her and she wasn't *that* charitable.

Benito squeezed her hand and she gave him a smile. Whenever he was as close to her as this, she had an awfully hard time remembering those hundred dislikable traits of his . . . or even one of them, for that matter.

She glanced at her father again, but he apparently wasn't in any hurry to get started—even though Sam was in obvious pain and needed a doctor. Or maybe *because* Sam was in obvious pain and needed a doctor. Could be she'd inherited her lack of charity from her father.

Finally, Mac stopped pacing and stood scowling down at Sam. "So," he snapped, "it was Dean Cooper who came up with the plan to kill Zoe and me for my estate, huh?"

Sam nodded.

"And when he suggested it, you just went right along with it. Figured it was a damned good idea, huh?"

"I . . . no . . . I didn't really like it at first. But Cooper, he said . . ."

"He said what!"

"He said you deserved it."

"What?" Mac yelled.

"Dad," Zoe said quietly, "calm down."

The way her father glared at her, before focusing on Sam again, made her decide to keep quiet and listen.

"I deserved it," Mac snapped. "And just exactly what did I do to deserve it?"

"You know."

"Dammit, Johnson, I don't know! But I intend to. Even if I have to break your other arm to get you to tell me. So start talking."

"Your South American deal," Sam muttered.

"What deal? You mean our salvage down there?"

"Sure," Sam said with a snort. "Some salvage."

"And what's that supposed to mean? There was nothing wrong with our operation. If it hadn't been for those damned revolutionaries—"

"Sure," Sam said again.

"Johnson, you've got three seconds to tell me what that *sure* is about."

"What's it about? What it's about is screwing people, Captain. Maybe you fooled your old crew. Guess you've had them fooled for years. But Cooper and me... we knew you got paid off."

"What?" Mac yelled.

"Cooper figured it out, and when he told me...well, it made real good sense. We knew you wouldn't have let those guys just walk onto the *Yankee* and take everything. Not unless they paid you off."

"Or unless I knew they'd have killed all of us if I didn't cooperate!"

"Sure," Sam muttered. "You put on a good act, but we didn't buy it. We wouldn't of cared, though. Not if you'd of given the crew a fair share. But just keeping it all for yourself—that's why Cooper said you deserved what we were doing. He said if you wouldn't give us a share, fair and square, then we should get one whatever way we could.''

"Good God," Mac said. "You really believed I cheated the men!"

"Sure. The Lone Ranger said . . . I mean—"

"Who?"

"Nothing." Sam glanced over at Benito, saying, "You're from Mexico. Does the word *tonto* mean anything in Spanish?"

"Yeah, it means foolish."

"Foolish . . . or stupid?"

"Right. Or ignorant. Why?"

"Nothing," Sam muttered. "Just something I figured was maybe a dumb joke."

Zoe wouldn't have imagined he could possibly have looked any more miserable, but he suddenly did.

"I can't believe you thought I'd do something like that," Mac was muttering. "Can't believe you'd think I would hold out on my own men. And to try to kill Zoe and me? When you and Cooper were the newest crew? Didn't you know my will said you'd get the smallest share if I died?"

"Better than nothing. We weren't greedy—just wanted what was owed us. Besides, we figured on grabbing some of the *Grifon*'s treasure for ourselves . . . in the confusion after you were dead."

Mac stood shaking his head. "So that was why. And all those things that happened to Zoe . . . ?"

"Cooper thought them up. He was the brains. Least he always kept telling me he was."

"He spread that mayonnaise, didn't he?" Benito said. "And he tossed the meat overboard. You were down diving when that happened."

"Yeah, Cooper did it. The only thing I did was rig Zoe's diving gear. But Cooper thought that up, too."

"Trying to smother me, though," Zoe whispered, almost unable to force the words out. "That was your idea."

Sam stared down at the floor, not answering until Mac roared, "Your idea, Johnson?"

"Yeah, yeah, my idea. With Cooper gone I figured why did I need him? Why couldn't I just finish up the plan myself...get my share? I'm not stupid, you know. If that damned bird hadn't—"

"I've heard enough," Mac snapped. "Let's go. I'm locking you in the strong room until the police come to collect you."

"Just one other thing," Benito said. "What about that jewelry Cooper had?"

Sam looked at him blankly.

"The rings," Benito pressed. "And the earrings."

"Cooper didn't wear earrings. He thought men wearing earrings looked like pansies."

"You mean he never said anything about any jewelry to you? Never mentioned the name El Gato?"

Sam shook his head, then winced, sucking in his breath. "Look, I told you guys what you wanted to know. So you gonna get me a doctor or what?"

"Or what," Mac snapped. "You can damned well wait till the police get around to it."

Chapter Eleven

The morning dive had been just about to get underway when the police boat arrived, so everyone was on deck for Sam Johnson's ignominious departure. Chicken Nelson had even found an excuse to come up from the galley, although he was feigning the same nonchalance as the others.

Zoe kept glancing at the assembled crew, certain they'd all end up cross-eyed from watching while pretending not to watch.

"*Más tarde, Señor Cárdenas . . . Capitán MacLeish,*" the officer said again, ignoring Zoe while he bowed and scraped his way off the *Yankee.* "And for your help, *muchas gracias.* We will take good care of your prisoner."

"And you're keeping an eye out for Dean Cooper," Benito said.

"*Sí,* all my men, they are keeping both eyes out. *Nos vemos,*" the officer added, giving Benito a little salute.

"You said," Zoe whispered to him, "Dean Cooper would want to get a million miles away from Mexico. As fast as he could, you said."

"I don't believe in taking chances," Benito whispered back.

"I've never seen a Mexican cop so damned polite," Mac muttered as the squat officer started down the ladder.

"That's what getting his orders from *federale* headquarters does," Benito said. "If I'd called the police direct, pretending to be a private citizen, I suspect it would have been a different story."

"You really don't care about your cover anymore?" Mac said, nodding almost imperceptibly in the direction of the crew. "They all have to be onto you after this."

"It doesn't matter. In fact, I guess you'd better fill them in officially—say over lunch? That way they'll be watching for more trouble."

Mac nodded.

"Hell," Benito went on, as if to himself, "the only one I really wanted to fool was El Gato and I didn't manage to."

"If we just knew who he was," Zoe murmured. Last night's excitement had left her short on sleep and even shorter on nerve. She half expected the mysterious criminal to pop up at any moment. Only if he did, probably none of them would realize it was him.

"We'll know who he is sooner or later," Benito said. "He's too damned stubborn to give up at this point."

"He doesn't have Cooper aboard to spy for him anymore," Mac said.

"No, but he'll come up with a new plan. He's probably sitting on Cozumel right now, thinking up something. Then he'll bide his time until you've raised enough of the treasure to make grabbing it worth his while.''

"Damned treasure,'' Mac snapped. "You know, Ben, I've got a good mind to pack this salvage in. It'll take us at least a year to raise the *Grifon's* treasure, maybe a lot longer. And spending all that time worrying about El Gato would give me more than fifty million bucks' worth of ulcers.''

"Mac, El Gato won't wait for anything close to a year. Like I said, he'll make his move once you've raised enough to make it worth his while.''

"And how's he going to know when that is?''

"I don't know. But he always manages to find those things out somehow.''

Mac shook his head, saying, "That makes me wonder even more if I'm crazy to hang in, Ben. So far, this salvage has been a disaster. Zoe's almost been murdered so many times that I've given up counting them. I'm suddenly short a permanent diver, I've got no photographer—''

"You have me to fill in for Dean Cooper,'' Zoe reminded him.

"I know, baby. And I appreciate your doing it. But hell, the crew are dropping like flies. Maybe I should just read the writing on the wall and give up. Hell, maybe I'm getting too damned old for this whole business.''

With the police boat well on its way back to Cozumel, Mac turned and motioned at Marco Vinelli to start the divers down.

Zoe watched as Marco gave them the order. The men headed to the gate, but Justo Díaz stepped out of line and started talking to Marco.

She eyed Justo, feeling guilty. She'd been so upset, after her diving gear had failed the other day, that she was sure she hadn't thanked him adequately for his help. Momentarily, she wondered what he was talking to Marco about, then she turned back and focused uneasily on her father.

She'd never heard him say anything about giving up the salvage business before. The *Yankee* was his entire life. If he didn't have it, he'd wither away.

And if he gave up on this particular salvage . . . she glanced at Benito. He certainly didn't want her father giving up. That would send the *federales* back to square one with El Gato, and his worry about that possibility was written all over his face.

Seeing his expression tugged at her heart. She cared so much about him that she'd all but given up trying to convince herself she wasn't insanely in love with him. And if there was anything she could do to help . . .

"Dad?" she said.

"Yeah, baby?"

"What Sam Johnson said about South America . . . ?"

Mac scowled at her.

She knew he hated her even mentioning that operation but pressed on. "Dad, you know none of the other crew would ever have thought you'd cheated them. But they must have felt let down . . . not getting anything when they were expecting to, I mean. And Chicken and Marco and Sandy aren't that young, anymore. The *Grifon*'s treasure would let them retire in luxury when the time comes. Dad, you can't just turn away from this one. Not when we're so close."

"I don't know, baby. I just don't know."

While Mac stood staring out across the water, Marco Vinelli hesitantly approached them, Justo Díaz following him.

"Mac?" the head diver said. "Can we talk to you for a minute?"

Mac nodded and moved along the rail from Zoe and Benito. "What's up?" he asked Marco, hoping it wasn't that Justo Díaz was quitting. He was by far the best of the local divers, and if he left . . . well, that would be the final straw.

"Mac," Marco said, "Justo was asking me about signing on with us permanently, about taking over from Sam."

"I am a hard worker, Capitán," Justo said.

"Yeah. Yeah, Marco has mentioned you are, Justo. But, see, my permanent crew always live aboard the *Yankee*. And you probably have a wife and kids on Cozumel."

"No, Capitán, I come from the mainland coast. I only came to Cozumel looking for the work. And I have no family. My wife, she died last year. And now, when I am alone in my house, I would like to be someplace else. Capitán MacLeish, you do not know how it is."

"Actually, I do," Mac said slowly. Actually, he knew exactly how it was. Twenty years and he could still remember the aching loneliness he'd felt after his own wife died. Even though he'd had Zoe with him all the time back then, he'd missed Melina every day . . . and night . . . for years.

"Justo's a good diver, Mac," Marco said. "And I think he and Danny would work well together. And it would take care of our problem."

Mac nodded thoughtfully. Maybe this was some kind of sign. He'd been feeling so damned depressed about things, then along came a solution to at least one of the problems.

"Yeah," he said, deciding. "Yeah, okay. I think you'll do fine, Justo. Why don't you bring your personal things aboard tomorrow? Then we can get you set up in the crew quarters," he added, extending his hand to the diver.

Justo took it, grinning broadly. "Gracias, Capitán. Thank you. You will not regret this."

"Good," Marco said, slapping Justo on the back. "Good, that's settled, then. Now let's get down with the others."

Mac watched them head along to the gate, then glanced at Ben and Zoe.

They were leaning against the rail, talking, and the way they were looking at each other...he swore under his breath. He'd have had to be blind not to have seen what was going on between those two and he sure didn't like it.

Not that he didn't like Ben. He was a good guy. But he wasn't a good guy for Zoe. She was such a free spirit she needed a man who'd give her life some stability—not one who'd be with her one day and someplace else the next. A man whose own life was sometimes on the line. If only her mother were here to talk to her.

Damn, but he wished Justo Díaz hadn't gotten him thinking about Melina. If Zoe knew how it felt to love someone and lose him, she'd fly like the wind from Benito Cárdenas.

Ben reached out and brushed Zoe's hair back from her face. Mac's stomach muscles tightened and he started toward them, his anger at Ben growing.

Irrational anger. Completely irrational. He knew that. But he could sure live without Zoe's falling in love with the wrong man.

He'd better start paying more attention to those two and do some interrupting if they started looking too cozy together. Hell, he seemed just to finish dealing with one mess when another one moved front and center.

"Well, I just solved one of our problems," he announced when he reached them. "I've hired Justo Díaz to take over from Sam."

"You aren't serious," Benito said.

Mac looked at him with annoyance. Ben's being in charge when it came to El Gato was one thing, but who got hired as crew was none of his damned business.

"Mac, we talked about the possibility of El Gato using one of the local divers to infiltrate the *Yankee*. So we sure as hell don't want one of them aboard full time. What if—"

"Ben, knock it off, huh? I've had it up to my ears with worrying about who El Gato is and what he's doing. And Justo helped save Zoe's life, for Pete's sake. So give it a rest, all right?"

"Dammit, Mac, there's no point in being foolhardy. I'm going to call the police on Cozumel, have them check Justo out. At least we can make sure there's nothing shady in his past."

"Yeah, well you do that, Ben. But good luck, because Justo's not from Cozumel. He's from somewhere on the mainland. And there can't be more than eighty or ninety million people in Mexico, so I guess it'll only take a year or two to get him checked out.''

"Dad?" Zoe murmured. "Dad, what's gotten into you?"

"Nothing. Nothing at all. I'm just sick and tired of my whole life revolving around this damned sting operation that I didn't want to be part of in the first place."

Mac wheeled away and started for the bridge, swearing silently at himself for letting his temper get the best of him. But dammit, he wished this was over so he could get on with his real life...and so Zoe could get on with hers.

ZOE FOLLOWED BENITO down the ladder to the water, still worrying about her father. The stress really had to be getting to him. Otherwise, he'd never have started snarling at her and Benito this morning.

And even though he'd played Captain Kind-and-Reassuring over lunch, when he'd been explaining to the crew about El Gato, he'd turned around and started acting like Captain Hook again to her and Benito.

That had convinced her their joining the afternoon dive would be wise. Hopefully, her father would have chilled out by the time it was finished.

She adjusted her mask and slipped into the crystal water after Benito. They sank to the shoals, then started swimming over to where the divers were searching—pausing to give wide berth to a particularly large and unfriendly-looking stingray.

Ahead, Danny Doyle and Justo Díaz were operating the airlift. Rather than the noise of its motor scaring fish away, it attracted them, and swarms of them swam curiously back and forth through the diving site.

As she and Benito neared Danny, he switched off the suction and started checking the strainer to see if their giant vacuum had picked up anything of interest.

Suddenly, his entire body tensed. Zoe could almost feel his exhilaration. He had something good.

He held out his find to show Justo. Then, seeing her, he extended his hand, palm flat, in her direction... and her spirits soared.

Even with his mask on, she could see the mile-wide grin on Danny's face. And she could feel a similar one on her own.

In his hand were two gold coins. But it was the gold ring case, lying between them, that claimed every bit of her attention. It belonged in a museum. She reached through the clear water and took it from him.

After all those hours she'd spent poring over the *Grifon*'s manifest records, she immediately recalled the details about this piece. Intricately carved, set with three of the most magnificent emeralds she'd ever seen, the little case was part of a collection that had originally come from the Far East.

In early 1724, galleons had brought it across the Pacific to Acapulco. Then it had been transported over the isthmus to Veracruz and loaded onto the *Grifon* for the final leg of its voyage to Spain. But the collection had never reached its intended destination.

Benito touched her arm in a question. She nodded excitedly.

Danny had signaled Marco Vinelli, and the little head diver pushed through the water to them. He glanced at the coins, then stood gazing at the ring case for a moment before flashing a thumbs-up sign.

Danny gave him an *awright!* fist in the water and began indicating exactly where he and Justo had been vacuuming since they'd last checked the strainer.

Marco turned to Zoe. They held a hand-signal conference, figuring out the probable sweep of the trail of artifacts the ocean would have carried away from the sunken ship—the trail that would lead them straight to the main wreck.

While Marco gestured to Danny and Justo the direction they should follow, Zoe tucked the case into the collection pouch she'd optimistically strapped around her waist before diving. Then Marco, Zoe and Benito stood waiting tensely while Danny turned on the vacuum again. Slowly, he and Justo swept a few square yards of bottom sand.

They shut off the airlift once more and rechecked the strainer. This time, they'd picked up two more gold coins, along with a blackened chunk of metal.

Zoe stared at it, knowing the chunk had once been several silver coins that had fused into a lump over the years—and knowing that finding everything so close together meant they'd definitely discovered the trail to the wreck.

Marco signaled the divers who'd been raking other areas of the ocean floor and assigned them to work in sections around Danny and Justo.

It wasn't fifteen minutes later when one of the temporary divers began frantically waving everyone over.

Zoe hurried across to him and stood gazing at his find, barely able to believe they'd come on it so fast. But there, peeking up from the sand, only a tiny portion of its hulk uncovered, was part of a bronze cannon.

Not that anyone other than an experienced salvage diver would realize what it was, not when it was so heavily covered with limestone and copper oxide. But if they raised it and took a mallet and metal brushes to the rock-hard encrustation, it would look like what it had once been—a weapon ready to fight off pirates.

Marco switched on a metal detector and started across the area surrounding the cannon, moving warily through a growth of razor-sharp elkhorn coral.

He hadn't gone more than twenty feet before the detector started to scream. He bent down and began brushing sand away, raising a cloud of silt in the water. Shortly, he started to uncover a second cannon.

Zoe's heart began pounding fiercely. They'd definitely found the cannon site. And that meant they were practically on top of the *Grifon*. Those old cannons weighed a ton and a half. Even the sea couldn't move them far from the main wreck.

Marco motioned at Danny to bring the airlift over, and they started suctioning the sand away from the cannon. It was customary to raise at least one of them from a wreck, and Marco apparently thought this one would be easier to uncover than the first.

She caught his attention and pointed up. She had to surface and get a camera. Now that they were this close to finding the site, she had work to do.

But more important, she wanted to show her father the gold-and-emerald case in her pouch. If anything was going to make him start smiling again, it would be seeing such a fabulous piece of the *Grifon*'s treasure.

Benito headed up with her, and they made it back onto the *Yankee* in record time.

"Oh, Benito," she said, shoving her mask up. "Do you realize what locating the cannon site means?"

He laughed at her excitement and said he hadn't even realized that what they'd found was called a cannon site, let alone what finding it meant.

"Oh, it means we'll locate the wreck itself any time now. Then we'll position the *Yankee* directly above it and start bringing things up. The crane can handle anything."

"Even that cannon Marco's got them uncovering?"

"Yes. And there'll be all kinds of things lying in the sand around the wreck. And we'll use the bigger air-lift, run the suction tube down from the deck now. Moving the sand to another part of the seabed goes much faster with it. And once we uncover enough of the *Grifon*'s skeleton to get into the hold...oh, this is it, Benito! We'll be raising all kinds of treasure in no time."

She glanced up to the observation platform as they shrugged out of their scuba tanks and called to Jake, asking where her father was.

"On the bridge," Jake shouted back.

Benito took her hand and they raced across the deck and up the stairway. She was so damned high he didn't want to say anything to bring her down. But he couldn't keep from thinking that once they began raising all kinds of treasure, it would only be a matter of time before El Gato showed.

"Dad!" she shouted, bursting in on Mac. "Dad, look."

When she held out the gold case, Benito decided he'd never seen two people look so happy.

"We did it, baby," Mac said, giving her a bear hug, "we found the big one."

He released her from his hold and carefully examined the little box.

It had looked big in Zoe's hand, but Mac's dwarfed it. Even so, given the size of those emeralds, Benito knew it had to be worth a small fortune all on its own.

"I'm going down," Mac said. "I want to be there when we actually find the wreck. You two coming back down with me?"

Zoe laughed, saying the only way he could keep them aboard ship was by locking them in the strong room.

"Okay, I'll just take a minute to let the others know they're going to be rich men soon, then I'll grab my gear. Sandy will want to come down with us. Jake, too, I'll bet. Hell, maybe even Chicken, and he hasn't dived in years. But none of them will want to miss out on the fun starting."

"Mac?" Benito said.

Both Zoe and the captain turned.

"Mac, don't leave the *Yankee* without someone standing watch. Especially not from now on."

Their happy smiles faded, making Benito feel like he'd just burst a kid's balloon.

"Yeah," Mac muttered. "Yeah, you're right, dammit. I guess the fun's starting in more ways than one."

SANDY, CHICKEN, and Jake had tossed coins to decide which of them had to stay aboard and stand watch while the others went down.

When he'd lost, Sandy had looked so disappointed that Zoe had offered to take his place. Both her father and Benito had jumped on the idea, though.

Benito had made a remark about her presence not scaring off a fly, let alone an intruder.

"Besides, you've got a job to do down there," her father had said, pointing at the camera slung around her neck.

Darned macho men, she muttered silently to herself while they all made their way down the ladder. She could stand watch as well as any of them.

But sometimes, although she certainly wouldn't admit it aloud, being considered the weaker sex had its advantages. If they'd gone along with her suggestion, she'd have felt at least as disappointed as Sandy had looked. She really wanted to be back down on the ocean floor, be part of what was going on.

When they reached the dive site, only one of the temporary divers was still removing sand from around the cannon. It was resting at a steep angle, and so far he'd just exposed the top half of its huge barrel.

Uncovering it by hand was a slow job, but Danny and Justo were using the airlift twenty or thirty feet away.

That had to be where Marco was hoping they'd find the main wreck because, aside from the fellow he'd assigned to the cannon, he had everyone working in the same area.

Zoe took a few shots of the cannon's position, then grabbed a spare rake and began sifting sand with the others.

The afternoon sunlight filtering through the water was promising about two more hours of good light when Marco started signaling like crazy.

Everyone rushed over to him, and he pointed at a small area of dark wood he'd exposed in the sand. It was extremely old, severely damaged by marine borers, and just maybe the most beautiful thing Zoe had ever seen.

She closed her eyes in a silent prayer of thanks, then was afraid to open them again in case the wood had disappeared.

Finally, she peeked. It was still there. Marco had uncovered a few inches of the *Grifon*'s timbers!

If they hadn't been thirty feet underwater, she knew everyone would have been screaming and cheering. As it was, they'd begun dancing around like men possessed.

Even Chicken was doing an underwater version of a jig, and everyone was slapping each other wherever there wasn't equipment in the way and swirling their rakes over their heads—as if the tools were mighty weapons and the crew had just conquered the world with them.

Then her father gestured toward the surface, one hand shading his mask, reminding everyone the daylight would be starting to grow dim in a while.

With obvious reluctance, the diver who'd been working on the cannon returned to his lonely task. The others started back to work near Marco.

If the wreck hadn't been covered by sand, it would have completely disintegrated in the warm Caribbean waters. Even as things stood, its fragile timbers were like old bones. But gradually, under the watchful eyes of a million curious fish, bits and pieces of the ship's original shape began to appear.

Not many of the skeletal remains of ribs and planks were still joined. They were mostly shattered lengths of wood. But Zoe's imagination saw what once had been.

She pictured a Spanish galleon, somewhat less than a hundred-and-fifty-feet long, with a width about one third its length, and suddenly felt as if she were shaking hands with history.

It was a history she was supposed to be recording, though, so she began snapping shots of the bits and pieces.

She'd just focused on what Marco was raking clear when the fellow who'd been working on the cannon appeared in her viewfinder.

He started gesturing to the head diver, pointing toward the cannon.

Marco followed him over to it.

Zoe followed the two of them, and when she saw what the man was excited about, her own excitement level jumped so high she almost forgot to take pictures of his find.

It was pinned beneath the cannon, but he'd exposed the entire top. That was more than enough to reveal it was a small sea chest —maybe two feet long and a foot in width.

It was encrusted but completely intact, so it had to be bronze, like the cannon itself. That was the only metal that would be hardly affected by long immersion in the sea.

She couldn't recall a bronze chest full of anything being listed on the manifest, though. The minute she got back aboard ship, she'd check those photocopies she'd made in the archives, but she couldn't imagine she'd simply forgotten about something the size of a large bread box.

Marco was looking at her, probably expecting she'd know what was inside it. She spread her hands and shrugged her shoulders, then made writing motions and shook her head, trying to tell him she didn't remember reading any record.

He nodded his understanding, then quickly pushed through the water and collected her father.

She repeated her pantomime for him, knowing what both men were thinking. The Fleet of New Spain was notorious for carrying contraband cargo that had never made it onto the manifests. And unless she'd missed something in the *Grifon*'s records, that's exactly what they had here.

But finding out what was inside the chest would have to wait until tomorrow. There was no way even the entire crew, working together, could budge a tonand-a-half of cannon.

Then her father tapped Marco's shoulder, pointed upward and gave him a few more signs—a clearenough message to tell her she was wrong about having to wait until tomorrow.

Mac MacLeish had a curiosity at least as strong as the one that killed cats. He intended to reposition the *Yankee* over the wreck site now, instead of in the morning. That way, they could use the ship's giant crane to free the chest.

Half an hour later, the crane's thick cable was snaking down through the water toward them. By that time, everyone had assembled around the mysterious chest.

Leaving Sandy still up top, Mac made it back down in time to have the honor of wrapping the cable around the barrel of the cannon and signaling for it to be pulled up a couple of feet.

The cable grew taut. The barrel jerked, then moved slowly up through the water as the crane pulled it into an upright position, freeing the chest.

With the end of the cannon still securely held fast in the sand, Marco freed the cable and attached it to one of the largest of the metal-collection baskets—while Danny and Justo quickly used the airlift to remove the rest of the sand from around the chest.

Then the two of them tried to lift the chest into the basket. They couldn't budge it.

Benito and Marco grabbed the two other sides, but the chest proved too heavy for all four of them.

Zoe stood watching, hoping none of them would get a hernia and making a mental checklist of what might have been put into that chest, almost three hundred years ago, that would make it so heavy.

Finally, Mac removed the collection basket from the cable and gestured that they should attach it directly to the chest.

Once they had it securely wrapped around the four sides, Mac signaled Sandy, up top, and the crane began its work.

Slowly, ever so slowly, the cable hauled the chest up from the ocean floor and through the water. The crew watched for a few moments, then started for the surface themselves.

Benito touched Zoe's arm and gestured a question, asking what she thought they'd find in the chest.

She shrugged slowly. In fact, though, she'd struck all but one thing from her mental checklist. But if she was right ... well, if she was right, the crew's excitement when they'd found the main wreck would be nothing compared to what was coming.

Chapter Twelve

Zoe, along with the entire crew, crowded around Mac while he tried to pick the lock on the sea chest.

Benito hung back, leaning against the rail, watching the circle of people. Every few seconds he scanned the water surrounding the *Yankee Doodle*, seeing nothing unusual.

But what did he expect? That ten minutes after they'd raised the chest, El Gato would come roaring across the Caribbean on a jet-ski? Maybe with a high-powered rifle slung over his shoulder like an ocean-going Rambo?

Hell, even El Gato couldn't find out about something that fast. Besides, they didn't know yet whether there was anything particularly valuable in the chest.

He glanced at the crew again, glad he'd given up on his cover. He was as curious as everyone else to see what they'd found, but if he were still playing government archivist, he'd feel obliged to warn Mac to go slow and not damage the old chest getting it open.

"Give me a damned pry bar," Mac snapped from the center of the circle.

Someone passed him one and Benito grinned. He couldn't see Mac for the others but could imagine the captain's expression. Mac MacLeish wasn't exactly long on patience.

A second later there was a popping noise. For an instant after that, absolute silence. Then the circle erupted with whoops and whistles and screams of delight.

From wherever he'd been, Billy Bird flew down to the rail and began doing his best to out scream the entire crew. Apparently, he figured earsplitting noise was supposed to be solely *his* responsibility.

Benito started forward to see precisely what the excitement was about. He pushed his way through the loud circle, then stood staring down at the chest with the strangest sense that his eyes were playing tricks on his brain.

He couldn't really be seeing what he thought he was seeing. People didn't actually go down into the ocean and hoist up a chest full of gold bars.

Yet that's obviously what they'd just done. Gold bars the size of big bricks. And like the gold coins they'd recovered, the bars weren't tarnished or encrusted. In fact, they looked completely untouched by either the years or the water.

Danny Doyle was lifting one out of the chest, and having a tough time doing it, which made Benito wonder how much the damned things weighed.

They were maybe a foot long, about three inches wide and two inches deep. And with eight on the top layer, and that chest about a foot in depth, a quick calculation told him there were forty-eight bars. Extremely heavy bars. And gold was worth hundreds of dollars an ounce, so . . . he started multiplying but the numbers got too large to possibly be right.

"Benito?" Zoe said, making him realize she'd moved to his side.

"Zoe, is that the genuine item?" he said as quietly as he could, given the racket around them. "It's not fool's gold or something?"

She shook her head and steered him toward the rail.

"Then how the hell much is it worth?" he demanded.

"Well," she said, laughing, "we'll have to weigh each bar to know for sure, but the standard weight was sixty-two pounds. So that's about a thousand ounces per bar... almost forty-eight thousand ounces altogether."

"Good God!" His numbers hadn't been too large to be right, after all.

"So I guess," Zoe concluded, "we're talking somewhere in the area of twenty million dollars—give or take a few million. Not a bad afternoon's work, huh?"

"Twenty million dollars... but your father's been saying the entire treasure's worth only fifty million."

As soon as he said them, the words "only fifty million" began repeating in Benito's head. When the hell had he started thinking in terms of fifty million bucks being *only* fifty million bucks?

"That's the value of what was listed on the manifest," Zoe said. "But obviously, somebody on the *Grifon* intended to smuggle that gold into Spain."

"What?"

"Benito," Zoe said, laughing again, "*you're* the *federale*, here. You don't think smuggling is something new, do you? All the gold mined in Mexico officially belonged to the king of Spain. But in reality, about twenty percent of it was skimmed off the top. So somebody, likely the *Grifon*'s captain or one of the officers, brought that chest aboard as personal luggage. Then, one by one, he'd have carried the gold bars aboard.''

Benito nodded, but his attention was drawn away from Zoe by the sound of a motorboat. It was, a quick glance told him, the boat that brought the temporary divers out in the mornings and returned for them about this time each day.

"Hey," Mac's voice boomed across the deck. "Let's get these bars down to the strong room before you guys leave, huh?''

Benito looked over at the chest. The bars were stacked beside it now, and both the permanent crew and the temporary divers started hoisting them up and heading off.

The motorboat drew closer, the two men in it gazing curiously up at the *Yankee*, clearly wondering about the activity on deck. The divers knew they weren't supposed to talk about their find. But there was little doubt a few people on Cozumel would hear there was twenty million dollars in gold sitting aboard the *Yankee*.

And there wasn't the slightest doubt in Benito's mind that El Gato would be among the few who heard.

RAISING TWENTY MILLION dollars' worth of gold was definite cause for celebration. So after dinner, the *Yankee*'s crew had turned the base of the giant crane into a makeshift bar.

Danny Doyle had begun making tequila slammers around sunset, and it hadn't taken long for everyone to start showing the effects of the potent little drinks.

Jake the Rake was sitting motionless on a lounge chair, his chin on his chest and an empty shooter glass in his lap. None of the others had reached the comatose state, but they'd all grown far more talkative than normal.

Zoe stood leaning against the ship's superstructure, sipping the wine she'd opted for over those killer slammers, and absently listening to her father, Chicken, Marco and Sandy reminisce about the old days.

While most children grew up on fairy tales, she'd been raised on stories of those early adventures. Normally, she still loved listening to them, but tonight her mind—and her eyes—kept wandering to Benito.

He was restlessly pacing the deck, staring out over the dark water, a man obsessed with his job. She watched him, wishing he were even a bit as obsessed with her.

But that was a stupid wish. Even if he were totally obsessed with her, what good would it do? She'd told herself a million times that there was no possible future for them. Yet she seemed constantly to be forgetting the fact.

Once El Gato had made his move, though, Benito would be gone. So she should never have let herself... But it was too late to think of should haves or shouldn't haves. What was done was done, and the way she felt was the way she felt. It was just too damned bad for her that the way she felt was so strong it hurt.

Benito glanced over and caught her gaze... held it in the dim light of mid-deck.

For a minute she didn't move. Then she put down her almost-empty glass and wandered over to him.

He smiled at her, making her pulse begin to race, and said, "How about a walk?"

She nodded.

They started slowly down the deck, away from the others, walked passed her dark cabin window and stopped at the bow of the ship. There, except for the glow from the white recognition light, warning other vessels of the *Yankee*'s position, the moon provided the only illumination.

Benito took her hands in his and stood gazing at her again.

Looking at him almost made her cry. *Her*, Zoe MacLeish, a woman who practically never cried. But she wished so much that there was some way—

"What are you thinking?" he murmured.

She shrugged, knowing there was *no* way, and therefore no point to a discussion about it. "What are *you* thinking?" she said.

"Well...I was wondering if you'd like to make a deal with me."

"Oh? What sort of deal?"

"Well, I was wondering if, when this is over, I could come up to California. I've got some vacation time, and I was thinking maybe we could spend it together...but not on the *Yankee* with your father. I've been getting the feeling he's decided the worst thing he ever did was ask me to stick close to you."

About halfway through what Benito was saying, Zoe had begun having trouble breathing. *Breathless*...that was it. His words had made her kind of breathless.

He had to be thinking that maybe there *was* some way. She had no idea what it could be, but if he thought maybe there was...

She stopped thinking. There was something she'd much rather be doing, so she wrapped her arms around his neck and kissed him until she was *entirely* breathless—so entirely that she had to come up for air.

He stood holding her, grinning down, finally saying, "Was that a yes?"

"Absolutely," she said, drawing his lips to hers once more. He had the most delicious lips in the entire world. And the way his body was pressing against hers, strong and warm and masculine, sent hot shivers up her spine.

All she could think about was making love to him again. And with her cabin right there. . . .

"Zoe?" he whispered, his mouth still almost on hers.

"Mmm," she murmured, certain he was thinking exactly what she was.

"Zoe, aren't you going to ask about the other part of the deal?"

"Deal?"

"Uh-huh," he said, easing back a little. "After I catch El Gato, I come to California."

"Mmm . . . terrific deal . . . I love it."

"Good . . . good . . . but there's the other part."

"What other part?" she asked, feeling a tiny twinge of annoyance. She didn't want to stand here talking about some dumb deal. She wanted to make love.

"Well . . . the part where you go back to California tomorrow and wait for me."

The tiny twinge was suddenly replaced by a major stab. "The part where I do *what?*" she demanded, pulling free from his arms.

He cleared his throat.

"Dammit, Benito," she said, putting her hands firmly on her hips and glaring at him. "I went through this with my father. Then with my father *and* you. I'm not going through it again and I'm not going back to California tomorrow. Got it?"

"Zoe, that gold in the strong room is more than enough to make El Gato sit up and take notice. So it wouldn't hurt you to just—"

"Look, I told you before, El Gato is after the treasure, not me."

"And I told *you* before, he's never been concerned about anyone who gets in his way. You know what your problem is, Zoe?"

"What?"

"You don't worry enough about things."

"Oh? Well, you know what your problem is, Benito? It's that you worry too damned much."

"No. My problem is that I've fallen in love with you. *Really* in love with you, dammit. And once El Gato's out of the picture I want to sit down with you and figure how we can possibly work things out between us. But I'd have a damned hard time working things out with a dead woman, wouldn't I?"

"Yes. Yes, you would. And I'd have just as hard a time working things out with a dead *man*, wouldn't I? So I'm going to stay right here and help make sure there aren't any dead men. Not you and not my father."

"Zoe?" Mac called from along the deck, far more tequila in his voice than she'd like to hear. "Baby? Did I see you heading off with Ben? Zoe, I want to talk to you about . . . about mapping the wreck site."

"I'm up at the bow," she called back, still glaring at Benito, not at all sure whether she found him more utterly gorgeous to look at or more completely and totally impossible to deal with.

But if he honestly did love her . . . and she certainly loved him . . . despite that, though, she *was* sure about one thing. If they ever actually got around to working things out between them, she knew exactly what the first thing they'd have to work out was.

As soon as the temporary divers arrived in the morning, Benito took Justo Díaz to the crew quarters and waited while he stowed his things into what, until yesterday, had been Sam Johnson's locker.

Either Mac had assigned him the big brother task so he'd have a chance to check Justo out, or it was another of the captain's plots to keep him away from Zoe.

For the last day or two . . . well, actually, since he and Zoe had spent the night together off the ship, it had been damned obvious that Mac was unhappy at the thought of them together. But hell, Mac had nothing to worry about. After last night, Ben doubted he and Zoe would ever get together again. He didn't even know how he could have fallen in love with a woman who was about as easy to get along with as a rattler with a toothache.

He forced his thoughts away from Zoe and glanced at Justo. He still didn't like having someone joining the crew whose background he couldn't easily check out, but he was probably worried for nothing. Zoe actually might have a point about his worrying too damned much.

"That is all I brought," Justo said, sticking the last T-shirt from his athletic bag into the locker.

"Okay. Guess you'd better go pick up your diving gear, then."

"You are not diving with us today?"

"No…no, I think I'm going to hang around aboard ship for the next few days." *For as long,* he added silently, *as it takes El Gato to show.*

They headed out of the cabin, Justo talking about how happy he was that Capitán MacLeish had taken him on permanently. Then they stepped into the brilliant sunlight on deck and Benito froze.

"Is something wrong?" the diver said.

"No. No, you go on to the equipment room." He waited until Justo started off again, then strode rapidly across to the gate, his hand automatically checking that his gun was in the pocket of his shorts.

A yacht, a white sixty-five footer, sat not thirty feet off the *Yankee*'s hull.

Mac and Zoe were in the middle of a conversation with a fellow standing on the deck of the *Leopard*— the name written near the stern.

Zoe, who hadn't put her scuba gear on yet, was wearing nothing but her blue bathing suit and a camera slung around her neck. And the way that fellow was looking at her…or maybe Benito was only imagining it.

He glanced at the name *Leopard* again, turning it over in his mind but coming up empty. It was flying a Mexican flag, though, and bore local registry.

"Yeah," Mac was calling across, "come on aboard."

The fellow nodded, then swung off the *Leopard* and into the rubber dingy he had waiting in the water beside it.

"What the hell's going on?" Benito asked Mac.

"Guy's name is John Medeiros. Wants to talk to me about something."

"Yeah? And who's John Medeiros when he's at home?"

Zoe gave him a sharp look and said, "There's no need to be sarcastic. Everyone in the world isn't potentially El Gato, you know. John's uncle was Carl Medeiros."

Benito stared at her blankly. The name Carl Medeiros rang a bell, but it was a faint one.

"Carl Medeiros," she repeated. "The captain of the *Pegasus*. The one who was killed when El Gato blew up his ship."

"Yeah, yeah. Got it. But what the hell does the nephew want?"

"Don't know yet," Mac said. "Says he came down from New York yesterday, just to talk to me," he added as John Medeiros reached the top of the *Yankee*'s ladder and climbed onto the deck.

"Pleasure to meet you, son," Mac said, shaking the fellow's hand. "Your uncle and I were close friends. And my daughter, Zoe here, knew Carl when she was a little girl."

"Then I'd like to talk to both of you," Medeiros said, giving Zoe an appreciative look. "You're a photographer," he said, gesturing at her camera.

"Kind of."

"Me, too. Not so much stills, though."

There was something about John Medeiros that Benito didn't like. He was just an average-looking guy in his early thirties. Medium height, swarthy. Nothing to differentiate him from a million others. Still, there was something about him . . . maybe the way his open shirt revealed about thirty pounds of gold chains around his neck. Or, more likely, the way he wasn't taking his eyes off Zoe.

"And this is Benito Cárdenas," Mac said.

Benito extended his hand, but Medeiros simply looked at him for a second.

"Cárdenas?" he finally said, reaching to shake hands. "Benito Cárdenas? That's quite a coincidence. I figured I'd have to ask Mac about meeting you. I've got something for you."

Medeiros reached into his pocket of his jeans and produced an envelope with Benito's name scrawled on it. He handed it over, saying, "Some guy gave it to me last night."

"He have a name?" Benito asked.

"Didn't mention it. I was in a bar where everybody was talking about the *Yankee Doodle*'s find." So much, Benito thought, for only a *few* people hearing the news. "I happened to mention I was coming out to talk to the captain this morning," Medeiros went on, "and a guy asked me to bring this along."

"What did he look like?" Zoe said.

Medeiros shrugged. "Big guy... I don't know. The bar was dark. He was wearing a cowboy hat. That's about all I noticed."

Benito stared down at the sealed envelope, curious as hell about what was inside and who it was from. He didn't want to open it in front of Medeiros, though, so he just said, "Thanks," and stuffed it into his own pocket.

Both Mac and Zoe were looking at him, clearly as curious as he was. But when he said nothing more, Mac turned to Medeiros and suggested they go up to the bridge. "We can talk there while my divers are going down," he added.

Benito started to object to the bridge, then stopped because Medeiros was listening. But, hell, he'd like to call headquarters from the bridge, right this minute, and get them to run a make on one John Medeiros.

No matter what the guy's story turned out to be, his showing up the morning after they'd raised that gold was damned suspicious. But the radio room was nothing more than a cubbyhole off the bridge, so a call to Mexico City would have to wait.

Mac, Medeiros and Zoe started over to the stairs and Benito followed along, not bothering to ask whether Mac wanted him with them or not. He didn't intend to let their visitor out of his sight.

He trailed Zoe up the stairs, dying to suggest she put something on over her bathing suit, but knowing the reaction he'd get.

When they reached the bridge, Medeiros shot him a curious glance.

"Oh," Mac said, intercepting it. "Ben's with the Mexican government. He's kind of an adviser for this particular operation, so if what you want to talk about has anything to do with the salvage..."

"It does," Medeiros said. "Actually, it has everything to do with the salvage."

"Then I guess Ben had better sit in." Mac sat down and motioned the others to do the same.

Benito waited until Zoe chose a chair, then sank into the one beside hers.

"So... John," Mac said, "all the way from New York, huh? So what can I do for you?"

John Medeiros sat forward in his chair, hands flat on his knees. "Mac, I'm a filmmaker. Documentaries, feature shorts, that sort of thing."

Mac nodded.

"And I want to do a documentary on the raising of the *Grifon*'s treasure. I've already got a distributor lined up and the funding's in place, so it's a definite go. And I thought, if you wouldn't mind a film crew underfoot for a while—"

"No," Benito said. "Sorry, John, but it's out of the question."

"Just a damned minute, Ben," Mac snapped. "This man's uncle was a good friend of mine. Let him finish."

Benito clenched his jaw to keep from saying anything more. But even if John Medeiros was for real, Mac had to realize the last thing they needed was any confusion aboard the *Yankee*—or within miles of the *Yankee*, for that matter.

"Benito," Zoe murmured, leaning close to his ear, "Dad is simply being polite."

He unclenched his jaw a little. Zoe was right, of course. Mac wasn't a fool.

"I realize it's something you could live without, Mac," Medeiros was saying. "But we'd keep the interruptions to a minimum. I've talked to the guy who charters out the *Leopard* and I could have it for a couple of weeks. That way, my equipment and film crew would mostly be aboard it. We'd want some underwater footage, of course, but we'd try to stay out of your way."

"Look," Mac said slowly, "I'd like to say yes. And if it was some other salvage I was involved with right now I'd certainly consider the idea. But... well, it's a complicated story, John, so I won't go into it, but I'm afraid this just isn't a good time. I can't help you out."

For a second, Benito thought John Medeiros was going to leave it at that, then he leaned forward again and said, "Mac, do you remember my uncle's wife? Mary?"

"Mary," Mac repeated. "I haven't seen Mary in…"

"She said it was close to twenty years," Medeiros supplied.

"I guess she must be right," Mac said. "But I sure haven't forgotten her. It was Mary who introduced me to Zoe's mother. Carl and I were both salvaging around the Greek islands and Mary had been staying on shore for a while—had met some of the local people. Then one night she and Carl invited me for dinner. And when I arrived, there was Melina. And we were married a month later."

John Medeiros nodded. "Aunt Mary told me the story. That was why I thought you'd go along with this. See, Mac, when Carl was killed… look, the bottom line is that he left Mary in pretty bad shape financially. That's what got me started on this project in the first place. The film will be dedicated to Carl's memory, and the entire proceeds will be going to Mary."

Mac pushed himself out of his chair and stood gazing down at the deck below. "Tell you what, John," he finally said, turning away from the window, "I'm going to come out of this operation with more money than I'll know what to do with. I'd be happy to share some of it with your aunt."

"Mac, that's a real nice gesture, but Mary wouldn't go for it. The family's tried to help out, but she's too damned proud for her own good—just refuses to admit that Carl didn't provide for her as well as he should have. And if she wouldn't take help from family, she isn't going to take it from someone she hasn't seen in twenty years. But she went for the idea of the film. She sees it as a tribute to Carl, and somehow that makes taking the profits all right.''

"I . . . I don't know," Mac said. "How soon would you have to get going?"

"Actually, not until you're nearly finished, when you've got most of the treasure raised. It'll be pretty easy to fake the early months of the search and the discovery of the wreck. In fact, it'll be pretty easy to fake anything except the treasure itself."

"Oh," Mac said, looking happier. "So I could contact you in a few months . . . after the excitement's kind of died down."

"No problem," Medeiros said. "The only thing I need right now is a commitment that we'll actually be doing it. So I can set all the wheels in motion."

"Give me a few days, John. Just let me think about it, huh?"

"Sure. I'll be in San Miguel, at El Presidente, for the next week. Figured, coming all this way, I might as well take a little time to enjoy myself."

Medeiros rose and shook hands with Mac again, saying, "I hope you can see your way clear to help out."

"Yeah . . . yeah, I think we'll be able to do something. Come on, I'll see you off the ship."

"Nice meeting you two," Medeiros said, nodding to Benito and Zoe.

"See you again," Benito said. He waited until Mac and Medeiros were two steps down the staircase, then started for the radio room.

"Where are you going?" Zoe demanded.

"I've got to call headquarters. That story sounded believable, but I want to check on the guy."

"Well, that can wait. First let's see what's in the envelope."

For a second, Benito didn't realize what she was talking about. Then the envelope Medeiros had delivered started burning a hole in his pocket again. He pulled it out and ripped it open. The note inside was written in a masculine scrawl.

Federale,
El Gato told me who you really are. For one bar of the *Grifon*'s gold, I'll tell you who he really is. I'm at a dump called the Motel Papirote. It's near the south end of the island. I'm registered as Frank Holt. Bring the gold. Don't bring a gun.

"So much for the Cozumel police keeping an eye out," Benito muttered, staring at the signature.

"Let me see," Zoe said, grabbing the note.

"Oh, Lord," she murmured. "So much for Dean Cooper getting a million miles away from Mexico just as fast as he could."

Chapter Thirteen

Zoe hovered outside the glassed-in radio room, blatantly listening to every word she could catch of Benito's second conversation with *federale* headquarters.

She hadn't managed to overhear much when he'd contacted them after reading Dean Cooper's note, when he'd started them putting all kinds of plans into action, and he'd been exasperatingly tight-lipped about what they were doing.

That made her want to hear as much as she could this time, but between the way he kept lowering his voice and speaking in rapid Spanish, she was missing half of what he said.

She'd caught enough, though, to know that John Medeiros had checked out as legit. And having one less potential bad guy to worry about was good news.

But now they were discussing backup for Benito's meeting with Dean Cooper, and she didn't like what she was hearing.

Well, actually, she *did* like the part about them not involving the Cozumel police. If the local cops hadn't even realized that Dean Cooper was on the island, they weren't people she wanted to rely on.

But she sure didn't like the bits she'd picked up about Benito intending to arrest Dean. Or about the backup that would be waiting down the road in case Benito failed.

She knew only too well that *in case Benito failed* meant in case Dean Cooper killed him. That was the part she didn't like at all, the part that had her insides aching with fear.

"Perfecto," Benito said. He continued on in Spanish, and she continued on mentally translating.

"All right," he said. "So the yacht will be in position within the hour and my backup will have arrived in two hours. I'll be there then."

Two hours. In two hours, it would be four o'clock. So at four o'clock, or shortly after, Benito could be dead. Zoe glanced at her father, wanting to think about anything except that horrific possibility.

Mac was reading Dean's note for about the hundredth time, looking as if he were still hoping to find a clue in it that would tell them who El Gato was. But the only way they'd find that out was by going to the Motel Papirote and facing Dean Cooper... who had already tried to kill her and Benito once...who, given the chance, would undoubtedly try again.

"Good thing Cooper left his notebooks aboard ship," Mac said, looking over at her. "I mean, good thing we've got a sample of his writing. Otherwise, I'd have worried that this message was actually from El Gato, that *he* was the guy registered as Frank Holt. And I'd hate to think of Ben walking into a trap."

Zoe nodded. But hadn't her father realized how high the odds were that Benito would be walking into some kind of a trap, anyway? He must have, she decided. He was just hoping *she* hadn't. But she knew

Dean was hardly Mr. Straight-and-Narrow. He was Mr. Armed-and-Dangerous.

"One other thing," Benito was saying. "I'll be bringing someone with me. A woman. I want her to stay with my backup while I go to the motel."

Zoe's gaze flashed back to him and she wondered if she'd translated that wrong. She certainly intended to go with him—had even changed from her bathing suit into one of the two dresses she kept aboard ship. But she'd assumed there would be a major argument before Benito agreed to her going along.

"*Bueno,*" he said. "*A las cuatro.*" He hung up and walked out of the radio room.

"I'm going with you," she said hesitantly, still not sure she had that right.

"What?" Mac demanded.

Benito gave her a tight smile and said, "Don't you want to?"

"Yes, of course, but I didn't think you'd—"

"Listen, Ben," Mac snapped, "I don't like that idea."

"I'm not crazy about it, either," Benito told him. "But I like the idea of leaving her here even less."

"But—"

"She'll be a lot safer on Cozumel, Mac. Look, I've got no choice about seeing Cooper, because he might tell me who El Gato is. But for all we know, El Gato and Cooper are still in cahoots. And if that's the game, that note was just a ploy to get me off the *Yankee.*"

"So El Gato can make his move while you're not here," Mac said.

"Exactly. And if he does that, I'd rather Zoe wasn't here, either."

"Yeah... yeah, I see your point," Mac muttered, glancing at Zoe.

She did her best to smile, even though it was obvious nobody was fooling anybody about how they were feeling.

Only she wasn't exactly sure *how* she was feeling. She wanted to go with Benito, but she hadn't considered that might mean leaving her father to face El Gato without them.

"Okay," Mac said after a moment, looking at Benito once more. "Zoe goes with you. And you're leaving now? You want me to tell Sandy to get the launch ready?"

"Not for about an hour. Everything will be in place by then. There'll be a car waiting for me at the marina in San Miguel, and a yacht anchored within sight of the *Yankee*. It'll have armed *federales* on it."

Mac nodded, as if having armed *federales* within sight was everyday routine. And the news that they'd be there made Zoe feel better, but only for an instant.

If El Gato tried to board the ship while there were armed *federales* watching, this bit of ocean could turn into a shooting gallery.

She didn't want to think about her father being in the middle of that any more than she wanted to think about Benito facing Dean Cooper.

"So what do we do now, Ben?" Mac was saying.

"The afternoon dive has already started?"

"Just went down while you were on the phone."

"All right. We'll tell everyone still aboard what's going on. Then we'll get out those guns you've got stashed in the strong room and put them on deck. Once we've done that, just keep a sharp lookout and act as if you're not expecting anything unusual to happen.''

"And you want me to get a gold bar out of the strong room?"

"Hell, no, I'm not taking one with me. If I screw up, I sure don't want Cooper getting a gold bar out of the deal.''

Zoe closed her eyes, wishing it were possible to close her ears, as well. She couldn't stand listening to another word. And Benito couldn't screw up. He simply couldn't. Not when they were talking life and death.

THE WIND BLOWING through the open car window was hot, but Benito didn't want to use the air conditioner. There was something comforting about the natural warmth, about the gulls screaming above and the surf crashing only yards from the coastal road.

He glanced at Zoe, doubting she was even aware of the sights and sounds. She hadn't said a word during their entire trip from the marina in San Miguel; she had simply sat snuggled beside him on the car's bench seat, tightly clutching his hand.

He could feel the tension in her body—the same tension that was gripping him. But whatever happened when he reached the Motel Papirote, at least he knew Zoe would be safe.

"When we get there...?" she murmured, finally breaking the silence.

"Uh-huh?"

"I could go with you instead of waiting with your backup. Maybe I could help."

"Zoe," he said, taking his eyes off the narrow road and glancing at her again. "Don't argue on this one. I'm trained to know what I'm doing in a situation like this and you aren't. You could do or say something that would get us both killed."

"I . . . I'm just so terribly afraid for you."

"I know. But it's going to be all right." He focused on the road again, wishing he was certain it would be.

Not much farther along, he spotted what he'd been watching for—an old car on the side of the road, a crate of fruit and a cooler of soda resting on its hood.

Two men sat on the ground beside it, ostensibly waiting for customers. One seemed asleep, his sombrero pulled down over his face. The other lazily rose to his feet when Benito stopped the car.

"Sí, señor?" the man said, shuffling over. "You like to buy a pineapple, maybe?"

"I'd like to leave the *señorita* with you," Benito told him.

"This is your backup?" Zoe whispered.

The man opened her door, suddenly alert and all business. The other one shoved up his sombrero and scrambled to his feet. "I'll see you again in no time," Benito murmured.

"Oh, Benito," Zoe said, wrapping her arms around his neck. "If you don't, I swear I'll never forgive you."

The man cleared his throat. "You would like to get into the other car, *señorita?* It is not so old and dirty as it looks. We will wait here. The motel," he added to Benito, "is just beyond the curve ahead."

Zoe slowly got out of the car. When the man shoved the door closed behind her, she gazed back in at Benito with a stricken expression that made his throat feel tight.

"See you in no time," he told her again, then took off without a backward look. He had to concentrate on Dean Cooper now, and looking at Zoe was the easiest way he knew to disturb his concentration.

A moment later the Motel Papirote was in sight. Just as Cooper's note had promised, it was a dump—paint peeling, the odd loose board, chickens scratching in the driveway's dust. They scattered when Benito wheeled in.

There was only one car parked on the property and it was at the end of the units, not in front of a door. If it was Cooper's, he wasn't giving away his exact location.

Benito scanned the length of the single-story building, wondering if he was going to see a gun pointing out of one of its windows.

He pulled to a halt in front of the sign reading, *Oficino,* and went in.

The office was a small room—hot and stuffy without a breath of moving air. Behind the desk sat a fat man in a sweat-stained undershirt, talking to a woman leaning on a mop. They both glanced over disinterestedly.

"Buenas tardes," Benito said, then told them he was looking for one of their guests, Frank Holt.

"Número siete," the fat man muttered. His lack of hesitation suggested there was only one guest registered.

"Do you know if he's in his room?" Benito asked.

The woman shrugged, saying there'd been a *No Molestar* sign on the door all day.

"Gracias," Benito said, surprised the Papirote actually provided Do Not Disturb signs.

He started along the motel toward room number seven, watching for the slightest telltale motion. But all he saw moving were the chickens.

A trickle of perspiration inched down his back as he neared Dean Cooper's unit. He edged as close as he could to the building, pulling his automatic from his waistband and holding it flat against his thigh.

When he reached the edge of unit seven, he paused. As the maid had told him, a grimy No *Molestar* sign hung from the door handle.

The door itself looked paper thin. But the entire motel would probably blow down in a strong wind. Cooper could shoot at him through the wall as easily as through the door.

He clicked the safety off his gun. The tiny noise sounded like a cannon exploding.

Taking a deep breath, he ducked down under the window, then walked quickly past the door, stopping on the far side.

He reached back and knocked.

There was no response. Not a sound from inside the room. No human movement outside.

"Cooper," he called, his heart thudding. "Cooper, it's Benito Cárdenas. I brought the gold bar. It's in my car."

Still nothing.

Gun clutched tightly, his finger on the trigger, he tried the door.

It was locked.

He raised his foot and kicked it in.

THE AFTERNOON SUNLIGHT dancing through the windshield was almost blinding, but Zoe couldn't take her eyes off the narrow road. She simply sat staring out between the two men in the front seat.

They'd reluctantly filled her in a little, so at least she knew they had a truck blocking the road on the far side of the motel. And before Benito's arrival, the only car at the Papirote had been a rental they'd established was Dean Cooper's.

So when a car appeared, heading toward them, it would be either Benito's or Dean's. And if it wasn't Benito's, if he wasn't driving it, she knew she'd no longer want to live.

When a car finally came into sight she began to shake.

It was white, like Benito's . . . but she wasn't sure in the sun's glare . . . then suddenly she was.

She threw open her door, ignoring the yells from the men, and raced toward the car.

A second later she was in Benito's arms—standing in the middle of the road hugging him, half laughing and half crying.

"Hey," he murmured into her hair. "Hey, I told you I'd see you again in no time."

She gazed up at him, scarcely able to believe he was alive and safe, desperately wanting to kiss him. But his backup men had reached them and were hurling questions at him.

Reluctantly, she moved away a few inches.

"Cooper's dead," he told them.

Zoe suddenly felt cold in the warm sun. It could so easily have been Benito who'd been killed.

He shook his head at her, saying, "He was dead when I got there. Lying on the bed, shot through the chest. Wearing that damned cowboy hat Medeiros mentioned.

"Get on the radio," he added to one of the men. "We need a forensic team at the motel."

The man nodded and headed back to his car.

Zoe swallowed uneasily, feeling sick. She forced herself to try and listen to the conversation instead of thinking about Dean. But he was what the conversation was about.

The other backup fellow was asking how long Cooper had been dead.

"I'd say over twelve hours," Benito said. "Probably happened between midnight and two or three in the morning."

"El Gato?" the man asked.

"That's sure my guess."

"You think Cooper was actually going to finger him? And El Gato found out?"

Benito shrugged. "Could be. Either that or El Gato put Cooper up to writing the note—to get me off the *Yankee*. Then, once Cooper had arranged for it to be delivered, El Gato didn't want him around anymore."

"Benito?" Zoe said anxiously.

"What?"

"The note. If it *was* a ploy to get you off the ship, what's happening back there?"

"Let's go check." He took her hand and started toward the backup car, saying, "We can do ship-to-shore on the equipment they've got."

When they contacted the *Yankee*, when her father's voice boomed from the radio, Zoe sagged with relief. The two most important men in her life were all right.

"Nothing's happening, Ben," Mac told him. "Nothing at all. Your yacht's still here, but there's been no action. Over."

"Good," Benito said. "Let's hope it stays that way. Zoe and I will be back at the marina in an hour or so. Over."

"Sandy will have the launch there waiting for you. Over."

"Roger. Over and out, Mac."

"So?" Zoe said. "What do you think? Since El Gato didn't show, does that mean the note was all Cooper's idea?"

"Maybe. Or maybe El Gato suspected that yacht might not have rich tourists aboard. If that's it, he'll play things safe by waiting until it's gone."

"Gone? You mean your men aren't going to keep watching the *Yankee* permanently?"

"Zoe, you can't trap a man if he's got the trap figured out. And if we left that yacht anchored near the *Yankee,* night and day, he'd certainly figure out why it was there. They'll have to back off, and we'll use flares to signal if there's trouble."

"But...but then the *Yankee*'s still at risk. And right now Dad is—"

"Right now," Benito said quietly, "your father is as safe as he's been all afternoon. That yacht isn't going anywhere until we get back. But come on. Let's get out of here."

Zoe waited in the car while Benito wrapped things up with the other men. Then he climbed into the driver's side and they headed off, back in the direction of San Miguel.

Only a few miles along the almost-deserted road, Benito pulled off into a shady grove of palm trees.

"What?" Zoe teased when he cut the ignition. The expression on his face left no doubt about what he wanted.

He drew her tightly to him, kissing her so passionately she practically melted in his arms.

"You know what I wish," he finally murmured.

"What?" she teased a second time. Again there was no doubt what was on his mind.

"I wish we didn't have to go back to the ship," he said, grazing her neck with his lips. "I wish we could spend another night alone together."

"Only one other night?"

"No, not only *one*, but it would be a start."

She cuddled even more closely against his chest, listening to the beating of his heart, so glad he was alive and with her that she could scarcely think. "Benito...last night...when you suggested coming to California after you caught El Gato?"

"Uh-huh?"

His lips had moved to her ear, and his warm breath was sending such hot shivers through her she wasn't sure she could speak coherently.

"Uh-huh?" he whispered again, forcing her to try.

"Did you mean what you said?"

"Of course."

"It wasn't just part of another plot to try to make me go home? We could really plan something?"

"No, it wasn't just part of another plot. And yes, we could really plan something."

She started to smile, but his lips covered hers. Then he eased her down on the seat, slipped his hand up under her dress and lightly caressed her thigh.

His touch ignited a fire inside her.

The planning, she hazily decided, starting to unbutton his shirt, could wait.

ZOE AND BENITO HAD BARELY climbed aboard the *Yankee* before the *federales'* yacht sailed off into the sunset. Zoe stood watching it uneasily.

The temporary divers had gone back to Cozumel for the night, so only the permanent crew was aboard, only a handful of men.

She couldn't help wondering if El Gato would make his move tonight. And if he did, how would they fare?

What if he had a whole army of hired guns with him? After all, he hadn't been alone when he hit the *Pegasus*.

She tried to picture old Chicken and little Marco defending themselves, but didn't like what she was imagining.

Sandy was a strong man . . . Danny Doyle, too. But Jake didn't have much muscle. And Justo Díaz was an unknown quantity. This was the first night he'd be spending aboard the *Yankee*.

Anxiously, she turned away from the rail and headed along the deck to where Benito and her father were talking.

Benito gave her a smile that made her wish they really *could* have spent the night on shore together. Just recalling the time they'd spent on the way back to the marina made her feel warm inside.

"What are you talking about?" she asked them. "What am I missing out on?"

"Not much," Benito told her. "We were just deciding that the two of us will cover the late watches for the time being."

"Sandy can handle things till midnight," Mac said. "He'll be relieving Jake in a few minutes, and he's as good as I am with a gun."

"All right," Benito agreed. "Then, if you took over until four, I could relieve you."

Zoe looked out over the water that had grown gray in the gathering night. She hated the idea of either man being alone in the dark when El Gato, the Cat, might be ready to pounce.

"Don't you want to see what the divers brought up today, Zoe?" her father asked.

"Sure...sure," she said, managing a smile. "They raise anything good?"

"Brought up some great things. They were working around where the stern would have been and found a whole mound of stuff. Come on. When you see what's in the strong room, you'll be sorry you were off on Cozumel with Benito all afternoon."

The way Benito grinned at her from behind her father's back almost made her laugh. The last thing she'd ever be was sorry she'd been to Cozumel with him.

They followed Mac to the strong room. He fiddled, for a moment, with the large key ring he always carried, then unlocked the door.

Even after his remark about the "whole mound of stuff," Zoe was amazed when he flicked on the light.

He hadn't been exaggerating in the least. The divers had brought up a couple of cannonballs, nautical instruments, gold coins and a beautifully engraved gold plate.

"That's the prize of the day," Mac said as she traced its design.

She nodded. "It's part of the same Far East collection as the gold-and-emerald ring case."

"Mac?"

Sandy's voice made Zoe jump. Even though he was a big man, he'd come into the room as quietly as a cat.

He was standing well inside the doorway, watching them. "I'm going up to relieve Jake now, Mac," he said. "Any new instructions?"

"Yeah, we put some flares on the observation platform. Set them off if you even suspect trouble. Aside from that, just keep your eyes open . . . and your gun ready."

Sandy nodded, then eyed the stack of gold bars for a long moment.

Finally, he glanced at Benito, saying, "You know, Mac has the only key to this strong room. And when it's locked up, it's a damned safe. You think your El Gato could get in here?"

"It wouldn't be the first time he cracked a safe," Benito said. "It would just be the first time he cracked one with twenty million bucks' worth of gold inside."

Chapter Fourteen

Mac stood gazing from the observation platform to the deck below. It was well past 3:00 a.m., the rest of the ship had been asleep for hours, but Zoe and Ben were still sitting on lounge chairs, talking in the moonlight.

The breeze caught a strand of Zoe's hair and she brushed it back.

A lump formed in Mac's throat as he watched. Her hair was just like Melina's had been . . . and she had so many of Melina's gestures.

Sometimes, looking at his daughter started a flood of memories. Sometimes, she reminded him so much of her mother it hurt.

Slowly, he shook his head. The more he saw of Zoe with Ben, the more certain he was that she'd decided Benito Cárdenas was the man for her. And once Zoe decided something, there was no changing her mind.

If only . . . well, wishing Ben lived a quiet, dull life was pointless. In fact, it would be hard to imagine Zoe falling in love with someone who did. And Ben was a good man. So if he made her happy, that was what mattered.

If only...but hell, he knew damned well how much
Melina's parents had worried about her marrying a
salvor and living aboard a ship. Yet every day they'd
had together, they'd been happy.

Mac turned and looked out over the water again. A
bright starry night like this held no secrets. And all was
quiet. No sign of any boats nearby.

Maybe El Gato would never appear. Maybe, without Dean Cooper to help him, the Cat would decide to
give the *Grifon*'s treasure a pass.

Mac glanced down at the deck again. Then a quiet
noise made him whirl around, grabbing his gun from
its holster.

The shadow on the stairs spoke up quickly, saying,
"Capitán, it is me . . . Justo."

"Dammit, Justo, you can't go sneaking around the
ship in the middle of the night. You're liable to get
your fool head shot off."

"*Lo siento.* Sorry. I cannot sleep."

"Yeah, I guess it takes awhile to get used to sleeping in a strange place."

"*Sí,* I thought some air might help."

Mac nodded, putting his gun away.

"Capitán," Justo said, pointing out over the ocean,
"what is that? A boat?"

Mac peered anxiously across the dark water toward
Cozumel, finally picking out the distant shape. It *did*
look like a boat. A large motorboat, sitting low and
silent in the water, not moving.

"What the hell," he muttered, glancing back at
Justo.

There was a flash of steel, pain crashing into his
head, then blackness . . . deathly blackness.

"YOU KNOW," BENITO SAID, gently running his fingers along Zoe's arm, "I haven't noticed your father glaring down at us for at least twenty minutes. Maybe we could sneak off to your cabin and..."

She laughed quietly. "Just because you haven't noticed him doesn't mean he hasn't been glaring. When it comes to me, he's more than a little old-fashioned. And us going to my cabin would put him into cardiac arrest."

"Well... then I guess staying where we are isn't the worst thing in the world. It's so damned peaceful out here tonight I can hardly believe it."

"Uh-huh," she murmured. Although peaceful wasn't the word she'd been thinking of. Romantic, was. The stars, the moonlight, the gentle lapping of the water. And Benito beside her.

Being with him made her so happy it was scary. And every time he touched her, she felt a delicious little rush she'd never felt with any other man.

"Even Billy Bird hasn't bothered us," he said.

"He's asleep in my cabin."

"Ahh. Another good reason for me not to go there. But you should probably be asleep, too. It's almost four. I've got to go up and relieve your father soon."

"I was kind of hoping we could keep on sitting here forever."

"Forever," he repeated. "Zoe...?"

"Uh-huh?"

"Zoe, I've never really thought about forever... but this last little while, with you..."

"Yes?" she said, her pulse beginning to race. The only man she'd ever even considered spending forever with was Benito. She closed her eyes for a second, in a silent prayer.

"Zoe?" he said again, sitting up straight and taking both her hands in his.

She gazed into his eyes. They were saying he loved her, and she knew hers were saying the same thing to him.

"Zoe, listen, I've been thinking a lot about you and me. But the problem is...well, dammit, no matter how much I love you, I wouldn't be good marriage material."

Marriage. The word started echoing from her ears to her heart, so loudly she could barely hear what else Benito was saying.

"I don't lead a normal life," he went on. "I'm here and there, I'm anything but nine to five."

"I'd hate nine to five," she murmured. "And I've spent my whole life being here and there. I wouldn't know how to live any other way."

"Oh, Zoe, this is crazy, isn't it? I mean how would we ever... with you in California and me in Mexico...?"

"Once my thesis is done, I wouldn't *have* to be in California. I could teach other places. Or do fieldwork."

"Zoe, you don't think we should even worry about all the details, do you."

"No," she whispered. "Not any of them. I told you before, you worry too damned much."

"And you don't worry enough. So together we'd kind of even each other out, huh?"

"Right... we'd be perfect."

Benito smiled a wonderful smile, saying, "And we'd be positively crazy to pass up perfect, wouldn't we. So marry me, Zoe?"

She threw her arms around his neck and kissed him. Forever wouldn't be long enough to spend with Benito, but it would do for starters.

"I don't suppose," he finally murmured, "your father can marry people aboard his ship? In the middle of the night? Then we *could* go to your cabin."

"No. No, I'm afraid captains of salvage ships don't even get to marry people in the middle of the day. But let's go tell him the news."

She pulled Benito to his feet, practically bubbling over with excitement, and they hurried up the stairs toward the observation platform.

"Dad?" she called from halfway up the dark staircase. "Dad?"

When there was no answer, they took the remaining steps two at a time.

For a second, she didn't see her father.

Then she did and her heart almost stopped beating. He was a black shape, lying beside the railing.

Terrified, she rushed across to him and dropped to her knees. Tears began streaming down her face. Even in the darkness, she could see he was covered in blood.

Then Benito was kneeling beside her, quickly checking him over.

Finally, Benito felt Mac's neck and said, "His pulse is strong. That's a good sign. You stay here and try to wake him up."

"But—"

"Zoe, I know what I'm talking about. It's important to wake him up."

"Benito..." Her voice trailed into the night. He was already gone. All that remained was the sound of his footsteps, racing down the stairs, and the sound of her heart pounding with fear.

Benito hit the deck running, heading for the shadowy shelter of the giant crane. Mac had still been wearing his gun, but his key ring was gone. So El Gato had access to the strong room. But exactly how was he playing this?

Not thirty seconds after he'd reached the crane, Benito spotted two dark figures coming out on deck. Coming from the direction of the strong room. Each carrying something heavy.

He pressed himself against the crane, watching. The *somethings* were gold bars—even though they were gleaming silver in the pale moonlight.

"Only two more trips," one of the men whispered in Spanish as they scuttled across to the open gate and disappeared down the ladder with their treasure.

Benito was about to start over to the rail when a third man appeared. And this one he knew.

He watched in shocked silence as Justo Díaz crossed the deck and followed the others down the ladder.

Like Dean Cooper before him, Justo Díaz had to be working for El Gato.

Benito waited as long as he dared, in case there were others, then walked quietly across to the rail and risked a look down.

A large motorboat, its engine shut off, sat in the water below. In it there were only the three men he'd seen. But that was three to one. And no doubt three guns to his one.

"Hurry up," Justo whispered in Spanish, his words drifting upward. "I'll spread out the weight of these bars before I go up again."

Benito moved back over to the crane, thinking fast. Three to one. He didn't like the odds, but at least he knew where the three were. If he tried going for help, he might miss something and get crossed up. And getting crossed up would mean getting killed.

He stood, not breathing, while the two men he didn't know appeared at the top of the ladder and headed to the strong room once more.

How long would Justo be, spreading out the weight of those gold bars? Long enough for Benito to take out his two friends? He didn't know but he had to try.

Quickly, he headed along the dark passageway to the strong room.

The door was open. The room's light wasn't on, but the faint glow of a flashlight was moving around inside.

He crept along the last few feet, his gun ready... took a deep breath, then stepped in front of the doorway and said, *"Alto."*

They froze, staring at the business end of the gun.

Benito glanced toward the door handle and saw what he'd hoped for. Mac's key ring was hanging from the lock.

But during the second he wasn't focusing on the men, one of them went for a gun.

Benito caught the motion and wheeled toward the steel door, firing his own gun without aiming.

He yanked the door shut, then turned the key and leaned against the cold steel for a minute, breathing hard.

The odds had just evened out.

Hoping to hell Justo Díaz hadn't heard the noise of the scuffle, Benito made his way back along the passageway, listening for any sound, hearing nothing but his own breathing.

When he reached the deck it was quiet and empty. He'd lucked out. Now all he had to do was wait until Justo came up from the motorboat.

Silently, Benito started across the moonlit deck to the crane again. Once he reached the safety of its shadows...and then one of the shadows became Justo Díaz.

"Don't move another inch," Justo said.

Benito stood motionless, adrenaline pumping like crazy. His gun was in his hand, but Justo's gun was pointed at his chest. Maybe Justo wasn't killer material, though. Maybe he could talk his way out of this.

"Justo, listen," he said. "Killing a *federale* would be a serious mistake."

"No. You are all that is between me and the gold. To kill you will be no mistake."

"One question, then," Benito said, desperately working to keep his voice even.

"*Sí?*"

"Who are you working for? Who is El Gato?"

A cold, calculating smile crept across Justo's face. "*I* am, Señor Federale. *I* am El Gato. I have beaten you again. And this will be our last contest."

Benito stared at Justo, his heart racing. El Gato was definitely killer material. And there'd be no talking his way out of this...yet talk was all he had.

He'd been so damned stupid! Right from the start, he'd worried about El Gato infiltrating the *Yankee* by using one of the temporary divers. But he hadn't *used* one, he'd posed as one.

"How were you good enough at diving to fool both Mac and Marco?" he said.

"I was a diver for many years. Before I learned how rich a life of crime could make me." Justo cocked his gun. The deadly click made Benito's gut clench.

"And Cooper was working for you," he said. He had to keep Justo from shooting. As long as he didn't shoot, there was a chance.

"*Sí*, Cooper would do anything for money. He would even have betrayed me."

"So you killed him. Because he sent me that note."

"What else should I have done?"

"And Sam Johnson? He was working for you, too?"

"No, only Cooper. And that is enough questions," Justo said. *"Ahora esta finito, Benito."*

He heard the shot.

But the bullet hadn't hit him.

And Justo was crumpling to the deck, his gun falling from his hand and sliding across the smooth wood.

For an instant, Benito simply stared down at Justo, his brain not processing what had happened. And then he looked up.

A few yards behind Justo's body stood Zoe. She was holding Mac's Colt with both hands—still holding it extended in front of her. And even at that distance, he could see that she was trembling and her cheeks were wet with tears.

"Oh God, Zoe," he murmured, striding across the deck and folding her into his arms.

"Dad's conscious," she murmured, pressing against him so tightly he doubted she could breathe. "He seems so weak...but once I got him awake, I thought you might need me."

Benito hugged her even more tightly. "Zoe," he whispered, "Zoe, I'll always need you. Always. But don't cry. It's over now. We're okay. We..."

He stopped talking and simply held her. Her shot had woken the ship. The crew, in various states of undress, were racing out onto the deck, gathering around Justo's body and shouting questions.

Quickly, Benito told them Justo was El Gato.

"He's not dead," Sandy muttered, bending over Justo. "Want us to do anything for him or not?"

"Yeah, one of you do what you can. But more important, see about Mac. He's hurt. He's on the observation platform."

Sandy raced off without another word, while Chicken ripped open Justo's shirt and started checking his wound.

"I've got to get back to Dad," Zoe said gazing up at Benito through her tears. "What if he isn't all right?"

"He will be. I'll get on the radio. We'll have a doctor here just as quick as we can."

"Oh, please make it quick enough, Benito. Please."

ZOE SAT HOLDING BENITO'S hand, certain she could never be happier. Well, maybe she'd be a tiny bit happier once her father had that bandaging off his head. And if he wasn't lying here in a hospital bed, glaring at her while he decided what to say next. But *a tiny bit* was all the happier that she could possibly be.

After all, El Gato was in a hospital in Mexico City, under *federale* guard.

The other two, the two he'd hired to bring the motorboat out to the *Yankee* and help take the gold from the strong room, were already in jail, awaiting trial.

And Benito had been told his next posting would be in Cuernavaca, which had to be one of the most beautiful cities in Mexico. And it just happened to be the home of the famous Museum of Cuauhnahuac.

With any luck, there'd be an opening at the museum for an archaeologist. Or possibly, the college in Cuernavaca would have a teaching position.

"Married?" Mac finally muttered, still glaring at them from his bed. "Seems to me you're being awfully damned hasty. Marriage is a serious step and you two haven't known each other very long."

Zoe managed not to laugh at the gruff act he'd chosen to put on. She knew he'd been thinking for the past couple of years that she should be getting married. And she knew he liked Benito. He just wasn't too crazy about the idea of a son-in-law who occasionally got shot at.

But if he'd ever really believed she might marry a boring old accountant or something, he'd been living under a delusion.

"You only knew Mom a month before you married her," she pointed out.

"Well...well, that wasn't the same thing at all. Your mother was living on a little Greek island and not doing much. But you see," he went on, looking at Benito, "Zoe has a lot of unfinished business back in California. She has her thesis to wrap up, just for starters."

Benito glanced at Zoe and grinned. "That going to take you the next six or seven years of your life?"

"Mmm...more like six or seven weeks. Unless I hurry and get it done in a month."

"Well, that's not all," Mac said. "You've got a lot of future commitments."

"Right," Zoe said. "Let's see, I have an appointment to get my hair trimmed at the start of September."

"Very funny," Mac snapped.

"Come on, Dad," she said, smiling over at him, give us your blessing. "Wouldn't you like to have a grandchild or two running around the *Yankee*?"

Benito shot her a look of pure panic.

"I didn't mean right away," she whispered. "I meant sometime."

"A grandchild or two," Mac was saying slowly. "You know...well, if you're determined to go through with this, I guess a grandchild or two might be kind of nice."

"So there we are, then," Zoe said, quickly rising. "How about if we have the wedding aboard ship? With your blessing, huh?"

"You know, baby," he said grinning at her, "that might be kind of nice, too."

He extended his hand to Benito and mumbled something that sounded suspiciously like, "Welcome to the family."

Zoe kissed her father's cheek, murmured that she'd see him again tomorrow, and escaped with Benito into the hallway.

"So," he said, taking her hand, "just exactly when were you figuring we'd have this wedding aboard ship?"

"Well...I *do* need a little time."

"Hey," he said, his expression suddenly anxious. "You aren't thinking your father had a valid point are you? About us maybe being too hasty, I mean. And about your having a lot of future commitments?"

"Well...there *is* the Third International Parrot Convention coming up. It's being held in the Canary Islands, and I kind of promised Billy Bird I'd take him."

Benito stood grinning at her for a moment, then draped his arms over her shoulders and drew her to him. "How about," he offered, "if I up the ante on that lifetime supply of crackers I promised Billy? How about if I throw in a whole bunch of Cracker Jack prizes for him to play with. Think we could convince him to trade off the convention?"

"I think we just might be able to. After all, birds..."

She'd been going to remind Benito that birds really weren't very smart, but it was too difficult to speak while he was kissing her.

Following the success of WITH THIS RING and
TO HAVE AND TO HOLD, Harlequin brings you

JUST MARRIED

SANDRA CANFIELD
MURIEL JENSEN
ELISE TITLE
REBECCA WINTERS

just in time for the 1993 wedding season!

Written by four of Harlequin's most popular authors, this
four-story collection celebrates the joy, excitement and
adjustment that comes with being "just married."

You won't want to miss this spring tradition, whether
you're just married or not!

**AVAILABLE IN APRIL WHEREVER HARLEQUIN
BOOKS ARE SOLD**

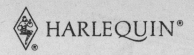

HARLEQUIN®

THE TAGGARTS OF TEXAS!

Harlequin's Ruth Jean Dale brings you
THE TAGGARTS OF TEXAS!

Those Taggart men—strong, sexy and hard to resist...

You've met Jesse James Taggart in FIREWORKS!
Harlequin Romance #3205 (July 1992)

And Trey Smith—he's THE RED-BLOODED YANKEE!
Harlequin Temptation #413 (October 1992)

And the unforgettable Daniel Boone Taggart in SHOWDOWN!
Harlequin Romance #3242 (January 1993)

Now meet Boone Smith and the Taggarts who started it all—
in LEGEND!
Harlequin Historical #168 (April 1993)

Read all the Taggart romances!
Meet all the Taggart men!

Available wherever Harlequin Books are sold.

Fifty red-blooded, white-hot, true-blue hunks from every State in the Union!

Beginning in May, look for MEN: MADE IN AMERICA! Written by some of our most popular authors, these stories feature fifty of the strongest, sexiest men, each from a different state in the union! Favorite stories by such bestsellers as Debbie Macomber, Jayne Ann Krentz, Mary Lynn Baxter, Barbara Delinsky and many, many more!

Plus, you can receive a FREE gift, just for enjoying these special stories!

You won't be able to resist MEN: MADE IN AMERICA!

Two titles available every other month at your favorite retail outlet.